Dachima Inaka

Illustration by Iida Pochi.

M000223859

2

Do You
Love Your
MOM
and Her Two-Hit
Multi-Target
Attacks
?

"Time for another adventure with Mommy!"

MAMAKO OOSUKI

Masato's doting mother. She knows little about games but has a lot of overpowered skills.

"I want to go to school!"

PORTA

A twelve-year-old Traveling Merchant. She is the youngest party member and plays a vital role in soothing everyone's hearts.

"...I've gotta get stronger."

MASATO OOSUKI

A high school boy transported to the game world as a hero. His OP mom constantly steals his thunder.

"I just feel like I'm losing sight of why I even exist."

WISE

A high school Sage. Her magic is often sealed, so she doesn't get to do much.

MEDHIMAMA

Medhi's mother. Obsessed with education, she gets in Masato and his party's way to ensure her daughter is the top-ranked student.

"I trust my mother."

"Mom! Why are you trying to answer?"

MEDHI

A cheerful high school Cleric who does whatever her mother tells her. But beneath the surface...

"Don't push yourself too hard! The scores don't really matter!"

"Losing is simply not an option."

SCHOOL SWIMSUIT MAMAKO

Mamako equips a school swimsuit, delivering a painful blow to Masato.

CONTENTS

Dachima Inaka

DO YOU
LOVE YOUR
MOM
and Her Two-Hit
Multi-Target
Attacks
?

VOLUME 2

DACHIMA INAKA

Illustration by IIDA POCHI.

YEN
ON

New York

Do You Love Your Mom and Her Two-Hit Multi-Target Attacks?, Vol. 2

▶ Dachima Inaka

▶ Translation by Andrew Cunningham

▶ Cover art by Iida Pochi.

This book is a work of fiction. Names, characters, places, and incidents are the product of the author's imagination or are used fictitiously. Any resemblance to actual events, locales, or persons, living or dead, is coincidental.

First Yen On Edition: March 2019

Yen On is an imprint of Yen Press, LLC.
The Yen On name and logo are trademarks of Yen Press, LLC.

The publisher is not responsible for websites (or their content) that are not owned by the publisher.

Library of Congress Cataloging-in-Publication Data
Names: Inaka, Dachima, author. | Pochi., Iida, illustrator. | Cunningham, Andrew, 1979– translator.
Title: Do you love your mom and her two-hit multi-target attacks? / Dachima Inaka ; illustration by Iida Pochi ; translation by Andrew Cunningham.
Other titles: Tsujo kogeki ga zentai kogeki de 2kai kogeki no okasan wa suki desuka?. English
Description: First Yen On edition. | New York : Yen On, 2018–
Identifiers: LCCN 2018030739 | ISBN 9781975328009 (v. 1 : pbk.) | ISBN 9781975328375 (v. 2 : pbk.)
Subjects: LCSH: Virtual reality—Fiction.
Classification: LCC PL871.5.N35 T7813 2018 | DDC 895.63/6—dc23
LC record available at https://lccn.loc.gov/2018030739

ISBNs: 978-1-9753-2837-5 (paperback)
       978-1-9753-2838-2 (ebook)

10 9 8 7 6 5 4 3 2 1

LSC-C

Printed in the United States of America

▶ Yen On
1290 Avenue of the Americas
New York, NY 10104

▶ Visit us at yenpress.com
facebook.com/yenpress
twitter.com/yenpress
yenpress.tumblr.com
instagram.com/yenpress

Prologue   One Boy's Progress Report

Are you getting along with your mother?
I don't think things are much different from before.
Do you have more chances to talk with her?
I have to talk to her when discussing strategy, so I guess so.
Is there anything your mother said that made you happy?
She said she was proud of me. (I'd like to erase this answer, but I don't know how!)
Is there anything your mother said that frustrated you?
When she insisted on keeping a tight rein on my allowance even inside this game.
Where have you gone with your mother?
Towns, fields, dungeons.
Have you helped your mother?
She always finishes battles before I have a chance to do anything.
Have you learned what your mother likes?
Me. (I wrote this as a joke, but again, I can't seem to erase it!)
Have you learned what your mother hates?
Maybe? She seems to have it in for mothers who treat their kids weird.
What are your mother's strong points?
Overwhelming firepower, good cook.
What are your mother's weak points?
She doesn't seem to understand the game or her son's feelings, and I'd really like to find a way to convince her to stop butting in all the time.
What do you think about adventuring with your mother?
Dunno yet.

He finished filling out the form.

"…Good enough, I guess."

Masato was standing in front of a pop-up window screen, checking over his answers.

He'd written a few things off the top of his head that he'd have preferred to correct, but there didn't seem to be a way to delete the answers. He'd been able to annotate them but wasn't sure that would really make a difference.

"Oh, Ma-kun. What's up? Studying?"

"No, not that… They e-mailed me a survey, so I was filling it out."

"I see…a survey? …Oh, is that about me?"

"One of the government ones. Gotta fill these out to get excused from going to school… Hey!"

He glanced sideways and found her beautiful, youthful features peering at the screen.

Her name was Mamako. She was Masato's birth mother.

"Whoa, Mom! What are you doing here?"

"What do you mean? I came into the game with you, remember? We're on a family adventure! Mommy is always with you."

"No, that's not what… I mean, why are you just standing right next to me? Argh! Look, just stay out of my space! Go somewhere else!"

"Honestly, Ma-kun. If you treat Mommy like she's in the way all the time, she'll get hopping mad."

"Will you stop saying that?! I mean, if you just considered my feelings sometimes…"

But his mother's cheeks were puffed out, and she was headed into a major sulk.

Their family adventure was just beginning.

Chapter 1 We Advance with Greed in Our Hearts! ...Wait, That Sounds Bad...

An earsplitting scream echoed across a grassy field at dawn.

"Aiieeeee?!"

A wolf monster's sharp claws swung toward a girl in priestly garb. A direct attack. The girl died instantly, and she soon lay inside a coffin.

"Augh! The healer's down!"

"Oh, crap!"

A warrior and a bandit, the girl's companions, rubbed their eyes in disbelief. But the sight before them remained unchanged.

There were four people in their party—the Warrior, the Bandit, a Shield Knight, and the Priest girl.

The Priest had been their sole healer, and with her down...

"I-if she can't cast Cura, we'll... Aughhhhhhh?!"

Mid-sentence, the Shield Knight was struck down by the enemy's fearsome onslaught. A second coffin appeared, lying beside the Priest girl's.

"Our tank's down! Rianimato them or...!"

"I know! An item should... Wait, I'm out?!"

The Warrior and Bandit both hastily checked their storage, but neither had any revival items. They didn't even have any HP recovery items. They stared at each other in horror.

As they did, the enemy attacked again. "Grrr!" "Gah?!" "Oww!!" Neither the Warrior nor the Bandit had much in the way of defense, and their HP crumbled away.

They were on the verge of wiping.

"Crap! What now...? What do we do?!"

"That's what I wanna know!"

There was nothing they could do. Except...

"...Ah! Hey, look!"

"At what? ...Oh!"

They'd each spotted other adventurers running toward them across the field.

Two of them. At the fore, a woman glittering gold in the morning sun. Behind her, a girl shining with pure white light.

Their bodies wrapped in gleaming garb, both women held staffs aloft. The woman's staff was magnificently bejeweled, while the younger girl's was of simpler craft, but both ladies had staffs equipped. That was key.

To the Warrior and Bandit, they seemed akin to gods.

"A-are you...Priests? Or Clerics? If you've got staffs, then you're definitely healers! You can use recovery magic!"

"Please save us! We'll gladly reward you! Name your price!"

Trying to keep the monsters at bay, both warrior and thief pleaded for aid.

The healer in gold smiled warmly.

"We require no reward. Helping those in need is only natural. Leave this to my daughter and me."

"Y-you're mother and daughter?!"

"You're so beautiful! You're angels! Goddesses!"

"My, that is high praise! But I suppose it comes as no surprise. Heh-heh-heh. Well, Medhi. Let us show them the power of angels."

"Yes, Mother."

At her mother's urging, the girl, Medhi, raised her staff.

"Conforto Staff! Unleash your power!"

In response to its wielder's demand, the function hidden in the staff activated.

Light rained down on all adventurers present, granting them a barrier that prevented status effects.

"How was that, Mother?"

"Well... I think this situation rather called for healing effects... but close enough. You did provide them a beneficial effect, so let's call that a pass."

"Thank you."

"But one must never be satisfied. You must always strive to be the best. You will become the greatest healer of all, a healer the whole world admires. The greatest healer in this world or any other world. Understand?"

"Yes, Mother. With your guidance, I'm sure I will."

"You will. Just as you say. I will train you to be the best. Have faith in me, and I will guide you. Let us proceed onward."

"Yes, Mother."

The mother walked triumphantly away, and her daughter, Medhi, followed dutifully behind, leaving the scene...

"...*Sigh*... Gimme a break..."

...and just then, someone seemed to whisper, "...Did you hear that?" "Hear what?" "Grr?" None present, monsters included, knew who was responsible for the whisperings.

So.

"...Anyway."

"...What now?"

The status-effect barrier was functioning perfectly, but the adventurers remained in critical condition, beset by monsters. What became of them?

Well, whatever happened, happened. May they rest in peace.

No one knew their fate.

Naturally, Masato and his party had no way of knowing, either.

When he woke, he found himself surrounded by darkness.

"*Yaaawn*... I guess I could get up..."

Masato reached forward, pushing the darkness in front of him as he sat up. The coffin he was sitting in dissolved.

Alzare always put him in a coffin. He was getting used to it. He wasn't sure he really should be, but there you have it.

Masato looked blearily around him, examining his surroundings. This was a room in an inn. A plain wooden interior, nothing in the room except a pair of beds.

The high school Sage who always forced Masato into a deep sleep was probably around somewhere, but he didn't see her.

"Guess she already went down to breakfast…?"

Or was she in the shower? He perked up his ears but didn't hear running water from the bathroom. She must have gone ahead.

"She could at least say good morning… Geez."

He'd better hurry and get ready. Masato stood and went to the bathroom to wash his face.

He had to do these things or a certain someone would start to gripe about his hygiene. Shaking his head at this, he opened the bathroom door.

A waft of sweet-smelling steam came spilling out of the shower.

"…Uh…"

He could see a woman through the clouds.

She was naked, wiping droplets of water from her youthful skin with a towel, making no effort to conceal her enticing chest, narrow waist, or anything farther down. This naked woman was none other than…

"Oh, Ma-kun?"

Mamako. Masato's mom.

Having accidentally walked in on his mother getting out of the shower, Masato crumpled to the floor, his mind and body obliterated in a single instant. He began to decompose.

"M-Ma-kun? What's wrong?"

"Oh, y'know…just…everything…"

This was wrong. This wasn't how things were supposed to be.

This sort of surprise fan service was supposed to allow him to catch a naughty glimpse of the heroine.

But all he got was an eyeful of his mom.

"*Sigh*… What's the point…? If it was Wise—not that I want *that*, but if it was—then at least I'd know how to handle the situation…"

"Wise? Oh, Wise…!"

No sooner had the word left Mamako's mouth...

...than Wise appeared in the bathroom, a towel wrapped tightly around her body. Like she'd used a teleportation spell.

"Sorry for the wait, Mamako! I brought a change of clothes from your room. Wait... Huh?!"

Wise had, naturally, locked her gaze on Masato. And was starting to freak out.

Before she had a chance, though, Masato yelled back, "Wise, what the heck? What are you doing?"

"Huh? Wh-what...? I was taking a shower with Mamako, and she forgot to bring a change of clothes, so I went to get them."

"Gimme a break! Why would you do any of that? How could you not be here? You've ruined the whole thing! God, you're a constant disappointment!"

"Umm... What? Why am I the villain here? How'd you make it sound like I should be apologizing? Um... Then...sorry? I guess?"

Thoroughly confused, Wise bowed her head. As she did...

Well, she didn't have much holding the towel up in the first place, so when she bent over, it loosened and fell right off her.

Exposing every inch of the high school Sage to Masato's eyes.

Thus, the world was restored to its natural order.

"Ah... Hey?!"

"Yes! This! This is how things should be! Maybe your thighs are a little thick and you're totally flat chested, but still! Or... Right, not the time for that, is it?"

Masato catching a glimpse of her meant only one thing. Punishment.

He slowly closed the door, as if saying, "Take your time."

But inside he heard the familiar chant. "...*Spara la magia*..." Wise was getting ready to cast.

Before she could, there was a knock at the door. Outside was...

"Good morning! Masato! Wise! Are you up?"

"Oh, Porta!" Masato called. "Perfect timing! Come on in! It's a bit of an emergency."

"It is? O-okay...!"

A young girl with a shoulder bag came running into the room.

She was a Traveling Merchant named Porta. With the items she carried, he might successfully extract himself from this predicament.

"Thanks, Porta. Can I grab a magic seal item from you real quick? I have an urgent need to seal the magic of a certain devil whose magic only works properly on party members."

"Magic seal item, right? Got it! Oh, but...magic seal items don't seal magic that's already activated."

"Uh... Already activated?"

Masato had not yet been set on fire, frozen, or blown up...but his punishment had already begun.

He looked down at his feet and saw a portal yawning beneath them, one clearly leading to some cryptic void or other dimension.

He began sinking slowly into it, like he was caught in a bottomless marsh.

"Um... Wise. Wise! What spell is this?"

"A spell to throw you into another dimension. Have fun! Geez, why do my spells have such a high success rate only when cast on Masato? They're like one hundred percent with him! It's sooo satisfying. Heh-heh-heh."

Based on the laughter echoing through the door, she wasn't prepared to cancel it.

"...This is gonna be a rough one."

Masato was dragged through the portal, his existence vanishing from the world.

FIN

Masato was no more.

But whether you died or ceased to exist, revival spells and items could easily bring you back. This was how the game worked.

So let's just forget any of that ever happened.

"All right, everyone, sit down. It's time for breakfast! Hands together!"

""""Thanks for the food!"""""

They were on the first floor of the inn, in a dining room for guests, enjoying their morning meal.

The room reeked of European romanticism, with an elegant table laid for just a few people. Only Masato's party had stayed here the previous night, so they had the place to themselves.

"This miso soup really gets me going! Without it, my magic just isn't the same! I'd go so far as to say my MP pool is based on miso!"

"I think my Item Creation success rate has gone up since I started eating Mama's breakfasts! I would like another helping of rice! May I?"

"Of course! We have plenty. Eat as much as you like. You too, Ma-kun!"

"Uh, sure..."

Breakfast with everyone, sitting around a steaming-hot pot of rice.

One glance around and you'd think this was your typical European fantasy MMO inn (because it was). Outside the window, the street was bustling with warriors and mages.

Yet the table itself was filled with rice, miso soup, fried fish, and seasoned seaweed. And everyone was eating with chopsticks.

What are we even doing? Masato couldn't help wondering. It was a real problem for him.

It wasn't like everything about the situation bothered him. Eating a familiar Japanese breakfast was a great comfort, even inside this fantasy game. It kept him in perfect health, after all. So even Masato was disinclined to gripe about it all that much.

Yet however disinclined he might be...

I dunno...

If he had to put a finger on what was bugging him, it would have to be her. Her very presence here, her every action, word, and gesture.

"Oh, Ma-kun, what is it? Something you want to say to Mommy?"

"...No, not really."

He'd merely glanced over at her, and she'd noticed instantly. He was forced to answer evasively and turn his attention back to his food.

Once breakfast was done…

"Well, time to clean up!"

"I can help! Masato, Wise, you can leave it to us!"

Mamako simply would not allow anything to get between her and housework, while Porta was always eager to help with anything she could. The two of them gathered up the dishes and disappeared into the kitchen.

"Thanks!" "Likewise!"

It wasn't that Masato and Wise were against helping, but it would never do to get in Porta's way, so they took her at her word.

Masato reached for his teacup. Sipping hot green tea, he glanced over at his mother's back as she tackled the dishes…and let out a long sigh.

Wise fixed him with a baleful glare.

"…Hey, could you not sigh like that this early in the morning? It's creepy."

"I don't see what's creepy about it. You don't need to be so mean all the time, y'know."

"Yeah, yeah, sorrrrry. But seriously, you're in a mood. What's up? …Or are you just letting yourself get bogged down by some dumb stuff again?"

"What do you mean 'dumb stuff'?"

"You know… 'Why is Mommy here with me in the game? I can't take it anymore!' Or whatever."

"Well…"

Masato couldn't completely deny it.

Thrown into a game world with his mom. That was the fate that had befallen Masato.

Being sent into the game was a pleasant surprise, and normally he'd be jumping for joy, but having Mamako there with him had the opposite effect.

But he knew better now.

"I get it, or at least I'm trying to. I know this game was set up for parents to adventure with their kids. I still have no idea how the whole full-dive engine works, but..."

"But now that we're in it, you can't beat the game unless you get closer to your mom... You know that, right?"

"I know the victory conditions are tantamount to death."

"So your only choice is to develop a full-on Oedipus complex, yeah?"

"Uh, I think I've got other options! I'm pretty sure the government agency running things doesn't expect anyone to go *that* far."

"Then just get closer to her normally and beat the stupid thing. Easy, right?"

"Easy to say, at least... But the whole 'normally' thing is what's tough... The goal's so abstract, I'm not really sure how to proceed..."

Masato poked at the air in front of his face, pulling up his status screen.

At the top was Masato's job, "Normal Hero." Like it was his duty to get close to his mother in the normal way and achieve a normal level of happiness. The job had been picked for him when they started, along with those instructions.

Personally, he thought that sounded way harder than saving the world.

Even if I try, there's no script or anything. I gotta do everything myself...

If we were to summarize his predicament in a simple Q&A format...

Q: Exactly how do I get closer to my mom?

A: Up to you!

Q: Have you prepared any events that might help with that?

A: As this is only a beta, no, we have not. We plan to include those in the official release.

Not exactly helpful.

A part of him was ready to throw in the towel, to abandon hope.

But actually, Masato had a theory. More of a hypothesis, really.

Like, if I could get in a position where I had to protect my mom...I think that might do it.

Not in a "I'll protect my beloved mother!" way or anything.

What he had in mind was more like his dad and grandma: watching out for the toll of her advancing years, quietly carrying her bags for her, checking that she was okay. That sort of thing always seemed nice.

Not to be patronizing, but if he could be the strong one helping someone weaker than himself out of the kindness of his heart...

If it worked that way, it would feel natural to him. Not awkward at all. If he tried that, he was sure he could pull it off. Totally.

The problem was...

...it didn't really seem like things were headed in that direction...

"Ma-kun, Wise!" Mamako said, emerging from the kitchen, the dishes done. "Thanks for waiting! Let me just get ready."

"Mama, here!" Porta said, handing over her gear.

"Thanks!"

She removed her apron and equipped an elbow and waist guard.

Then she slung two Holy Swords around her hips—Terra di Madre, the Holy Sword of Mother Earth, and Altura, the Holy Sword of Mother Ocean. And with that, she was ready.

"Well then, Ma-kun! Time for another adventure with Mommy! Yay!"

"Yeah, okay... Yay..."

Once again, Masato had to face the harsh reality.

Shortly after they reached the field...

"...Oh! Enemies! Careful!" Porta cried, her eagle eyes quickly spotting the approaching monsters. She hastily retreated to the back line. Porta was registered as a noncombatant account and was unable to take part in any battles.

Fights were handled by Masato, Mamako, and Wise.

"Right, let's do this! Prepare for combat!"

"Yes! Mommy will do her best!"

"Expect great things from the super schoolgirl Sage!"

The party makeup was two sword-based DPS units with an

all-rounder Mage handling offensive, recovery, and support spells. A handpicked elite unit up for any challenge.

Their foes were a pack of bugs and vermin, ranging from grasshoppers to rats.

The instant both parties perceived each other, the battle began.

"Ha-ha! My magic will end this in a single blow! *Spara la magia...*"

Wise was the first to take action. She summoned her magic tome, opened it up, and began chanting the words to a spell.

But the enemy was faster. A giant grasshopper got the initiative.

...Vvvvvvvvvv...

The giant grasshopper's wings vibrated, unleashing an uncanny noise.

Masato was unaffected. Mamako was unaffected. Naturally, Porta was unaffected.

Wise's magic was sealed.

"...Why...? Every time... Why...?" Wise said, crumpling to the ground, her eyes glazing over.

"It shouldn't come as a shock at this point! That's all you ever do!" Masato said, dashing past her to attack. "Which means this battle is miiiiine!"

Masato took a firm grip on Firmamento, the Holy Sword of the Heavens. The enemies were right before his eyes.

Firmamento was a sword specialized for fighting flying enemies, but it was naturally capable of defeating ground-based foes as well. The glittering transparent blade swung toward the giant grasshopper.

But sadly...

"Hyah!"

Just before Masato's attack connected, a feminine squeak far too adorable to ever emerge from someone her age echoed in his ear.

Instantly, rock spikes jutted up from beneath the monsters' feet, impaling and shredding every creature there.

A moment later, an immense number of water bullets, like a full clip from an assault rifle, riddled the monsters with holes.

By the time the fury of her multi-target attacks subsided, the only trace of the monsters were the dice-shaped objects known as gems. These were generated within the monsters themselves and scattered on the ground where they'd stood.

Yep. She'd beaten all the monsters.

"Look, look, Ma-kun! Mommy did it!"

Mamako had cleaned up. She was hopping up and down happily, a crimson sword in her right hand and a navy-blue one in her left, a broad smile on her face. All this hopping was making her chest bounce all over the place.

Meanwhile, Wise had stepped forward with utter confidence only to have her magic sealed, rendering her useless. And Masato had attempted to seize his chance, moving to attack only to have his efforts prove to be in vain.

"...Look."

"...Don't. She'll just cry again."

Mamako was quite proud of her two-hit multi-target attacks and her overwhelming firepower.

They never let the other party members get a hit in. Not ever. Not once. Anywhere.

It was hopeless.

Masato and Wise quietly sat down side by side. They'd found sitting with their arms around their knees was a great comfort when they felt like this.

Meanwhile, Porta scrambled around collecting the gems (which could be exchanged for money). Mamako was helping her.

As they absently watched them, Wise started talking.

"I've been thinking... I'm really screwed. I dunno, I just feel like I'm losing sight of why I even exist."

"What a coincidence. That's exactly what I was thinking... If we don't do something soon, we're doomed."

Mamako was unbeatable in combat. Masato never got a chance to shine.

This was a dire state of affairs. Not as far as the combat results—those went swimmingly—but the toll on Masato's state of mind was severe.

Essentially, Mamako made him feel inadequate. He was trying to

move beyond childish reactions like blaming her or lashing out, but at this rate there was no guarantee he wouldn't erupt again.

And…

The way things are, I'll never get a chance to be the one protecting her…

Masato believed that getting closer to her required tenderness and consideration. Or at least, he had a nebulous concept that was similar.

But to put those feelings into specific action required a good deal of self-confidence.

Everyone knows that it's better to be nice to your mother, to be thoughtful. But the power to do that and think *This is the right thing to do* was rooted in confidence.

And confidence stemmed from strength.

At least at first.

"…I've gotta get stronger," Masato said in a whisper. He let the words linger in the air.

"Pffft! 'I've gotta get stronger.' Hearing a guy say that with a straight face is hilarious!"

"Wh-what're you laughing at?! See, this is what really pisses me off about girls!!"

Masato spent a few minutes seriously thinking about whether the experience he'd gain from defeating Wise (who was still laughing) would be enough to make him level up.

Mornings were spent battling, earning enough money to live on. The daily grind for living expenses progressed smoothly, and when they looked up, they realized the sun was directly overhead. Noon. The party went back to town for lunch.

The town the party was operating out of at the moment was just a set of inns without a name. It lay on the road between the starting town, Catharn, and the capital city farther inland. Just a transitional point along the way. There were a few houses and shops, but it was mostly travelers passing through, which kept the place bustling.

So.

"So where should we get lunch?"

"Mm… Anywhere's fine. Just grab something at one of these stalls and eat on the Adventurers Guild terrace."

"Sounds good to me. They've got free refills there."

"Pay a set price and drink as much as you like! The more you drink, the more you save!"

"Well, savings are always good. Let's do that."

By unanimous decision, they elected to use the Adventurers Guild like one of those restaurants that let you bring in outside food. They grabbed some fast food from a street vendor and headed toward the guild.

The Adventurers Guild was an association that provided a number of services to adventurers. It had branches all over the game world, wherever you might go. The guild branch in this inn town was smaller than the one in the city, but it functioned the same way.

When Masato's party reached the guild, they found it full of adventurers. Burly warriors, robe-clad mages, people of all jobs.

"Pretty crowded…"

"It *is* noon, after all… Any empty seats…?"

"Oh, looks like that table just opened up."

"I'll nab it for us! Leave it to me!"

Before they could say anything, Porta's tiny body slipped off through the crowd, claiming the empty table. She was as quick as she was cute.

Thanks to Porta, they had seats, so the rest of them got drinks and joined her.

"Well, everyone, let's dig in."

""""Thanks for the food!"""""

The room was loud but not too loud. It was an enjoyable lunch.

Fortunately, the seats they'd found were right next to the quest board. As Masato munched on his burger, he glanced over the posted quests.

The tasks on the board ranged from eliminating specific monsters to delivering specific items; lots of generic stuff.

Don't suppose there's a quest that could somehow power up just us kids...

Normal quests would spread the experience evenly among the entire party, so Mamako would be strengthened just as much as them. At this rate, they would never catch up.

Which meant they had to focus on the rewards. A quest that granted boost items that only the kids could equip, or items that would work only on Masato himself, that would be ideal.

He looked around for anything like that...

"...Mm?"

And his eyes locked on one request.

RECRUITING PARTICIPANTS FOR SCHOOL TRIAL ACTIVITIES.

An unusual request. Like the header suggested, they'd be going to school. They'd be students attending that school.

Anyone accepting this quest would be required to take classes in return for the SP used to raise stats and learn skills. And it said these SP could be exchanged for items that would strengthen the children.

That was it! That was exactly what he was looking for.

"This! This is it!"

He wasn't supposed to rip the quest posting off the board, but he did anyway, and he slammed it down in the middle of the table, gesturing at it.

"Guys, look at this! Isn't it perfect? We should definitely do this! C'mon!"

"Wh-what the...? Is this...? Huh? School?"

"Attend school, take classes, and get SP...?"

"Um, Ma-kun. What was SP again? Mommy can't remember."

"Remember how you get a few points every time we level up? Those."

"Oh...right... I didn't really understand it, so I just let them be..."

"Whaaat?! We've gone up a bunch of levels and you haven't used any SP?! Yet you're still that strong?!"

All mothers are notorious for hoarding points for ages without ever using them. You've just gotta let them do it their way. No point in arguing. That aside...

"But doesn't it sound great? This could be a huge win for us," Masato insisted.

He was certain this would pay off for him, so he was getting a little intense.

"Hmm... I'll pass," Wise said, looking bored.

"Are you kidding? You can't *not* do this! Don't be a doofus!"

"What's a doofus? It sounds kinda cute, so maybe I'll let it slide... Anyway, I just thought..."

"...Thought what?"

"I mean, we got permission to get out of school to play this game, right? So why the hell would we go to school *in* the game? It just sounds like a giant pain in the ass."

"Th-that's actually a pretty good point..."

The game they were currently doing a full dive in was being run by the Japanese government, and as test players, they were being excused from a number of obligations.

What was the point, then, of submitting themselves to those exact same obligations within the game? Wise was making a lot of sense, and Masato could totally understand her point...

"Um, can I say something?" Porta asked. "There's a thing I'm curious about."

"Uh, sure, what is it?"

"It looks like only children can join in this quest. So Mama can't join us! I don't think that's fair!"

"What? Really?"

"Yes! That's what it says!"

Porta pointed to the request. The bottom of it read, ONLY OPEN TO CHILDREN FROM ELEMENTARY TO HIGH SCHOOL. It was in such fine print that almost nobody would even notice it was there.

That left Mamako out completely. Only the three children would be able to accept the quest.

Since the goal was to strengthen just the kids, that actually worked in Masato's favor...

Or would it? They were a party, Mamako included. Even if it was his mother, it hardly seemed fair to leave someone out like this.

But…

"Oh, I think it sounds lovely," Mamako said. "Ma-kun, Wise, Porta, I think you should do this together!"

She didn't seem to mind at all.

"Um…? Mom, are you sure?"

"Of course! I don't see a problem."

"No, but… We're here so you and I can adventure together, right? So if we do something that leaves you out… I mean…"

Masato's expression darkened. He was starting to feel guilty.

Mamako beamed, her smiling face as bright as a sun trying to banish each and every shadow.

"Mommy thinks Ma-kun should be able to do anything he wants to. What's most important is how you feel."

Her unshakable conviction easily drove away his worries.

"…You're sure about this?"

"Yes. Don't you worry. Porta, you don't need to worry, either. If you want to go to school, say so. Just say how you really feel. Okay?"

"Unhhh… I…I want to go to school!"

"See, now isn't that nice? …That leaves you, Wise…"

"AHHHHHHHHHHHHHHHHHHHHHHHHHHHHHHHHHH?!"

Wise's face twisted into an expression no girl should ever make. Eyes locked to the request, she suddenly let out a bloodcurdling shriek. This was Wise, right? It *was* Wise. The horror.

"Wh…whaaaaat?! M-M-M-Masato! Masatooo!"

"Would you mind not calling my name out? People will think we know each other. It's embarrassing."

"To hell with that! Look! At the request! Here!"

"Yeah, yeah, what is it?"

Masato wanted desperately to pretend she was a complete stranger. Wise's display of surprise was so dramatic she seemed on the verge of spraying snot out her nose. But he looked where she pointed.

At the space below the fine print.

Sample items obtainable with SP: Strength Stemma, Prevenire, Stuffed Animal, etc.

For some reason, this sentence alone was written by hand.

"Um... So what?"

"So what?! That's a Prevenire! A Prevenire!"

"You can yell that word all you like, but I still don't know what it is. I guess that means it's time for our item expert to explain. Porta?"

"Got it! A Prevenire is an accessory that completely prevents magic from being sealed. If she equips one, she'll never have to worry about getting sealed again!"

"Yes! I *neeeeeed* one of those more than anything!"

"R-right... That explains why you're blowing a gasket."

"Also, the Strength Stemma is an emblem that raises attack power. You stick it to your body like a temporary tattoo."

"Oh? Nice. I could use one of those."

"And—and the Stuffed Animal is also amazing! It raises your Item Creation success rate! I...I really want a Stuffed Animal..."

Porta clasped her little hands together, hopping up and down with excitement. She. Was. Too. Cute.

The exchange items gripped the party's hearts!

"I told you this was gonna be great! If we do this quest, all three of us can get the items we're after! All three of... Uh..."

Hang on.

The items listed as examples of what would be available were a little *too* specifically what his party members were after.

Hmm... That sure seems a little contrived...

It had certainly gotten all of them on board.

"Let's head to the quest location! Yay!"

"Prevenireeeeeeeeeee! You will be miiiiiiiiiiiiiiiiiiiiiiiiiiiiiiiiiine!"

"Wise. I think we've all had enough of your ridiculous hype. Please try to consider the feelings of your party members. Even Porta is mildly perturbed."

"N-no! I-I-I'm okay with it, just... Oh, the carriage is here!"

After several minutes putting up with Wise's obnoxious behavior, they were all extremely ready for the arrival of the carriage that carried passengers from town to town. Haste was in order, so they were taking a four-horse express carriage direct to their destination. All aboard!

Inside the carriage compartment were long benches, like a train. There were two passengers already waiting inside.

When Masato saw them, he found himself saying aloud, "Whoa... She's gorgeous..."

He was referring to a girl with long blue hair.

Her gaze was directed slightly downward, and seen in profile, there was a real elegance to her, like an aristocrat's daughter. Maybe even a princess. Either way, she was gorgeous.

She was wearing proper pure-white attire. At her side, there was a simple, well-used staff. Judging from her equipment, she was a Priest or a Cleric and would be focused on healing spells in combat.

Next to her was a grown woman with similar features. Presumably her mother. She, too, retained her youth and beauty, if not quite to Mamako's extreme degree.

She was wearing an extremely flashy outfit embroidered with gold thread, like a nouveau riche archbishop. Her staff, too, was studded with jewels.

But it was the girl who drew the eye.

An elegant, beautiful, young healer... That's what I'm talking about. That's what a heroine should be!

A girl like this deserved to stand at a hero's side.

Instead, by some terrible mistake, he had his mom.

If this beautiful healer joined his party, and one thing led to another, and she and Masato became close, that would be living the dream.

"Yo, Masato, what the hell? Hurry up and get in."

"Huh? O-oh, right. Sorry."

This was no time to be staring. With Wise poking him in the back, Masato hastily clambered into the carriage.

Masato's party lined up opposite the healer duo. From the front, Porta, Mamako, Masato (who'd wanted to avoid sitting next to

Mamako but had gotten pushed into it and left with no choice), and finally, the weirdo who wouldn't stop yelling "I'm coming for you, Prevenireeeeee!"

With all passengers on board, the carriage took off.

"Now we just have to wait till we're there."

"Yes... My, this carriage's gentle rocking certainly is soothing. It makes me want to take a nap!"

"Yeah... Wow, two of us are already out."

Wise had been screaming a moment before, but now she was sound asleep. On the other side of Mamako, Porta was having trouble keeping her eyes open.

Mamako put her arm around Porta, laying her head down on her lap.

"Hee-hee, Porta's fast asleep... Ma-kun, won't you join her? Have a little nap on Mommy's lap, just like the other day."

Mamako patted her thighs encouragingly, offering her lap.

Her lap was so undeniably comfortable that part of him wanted to just keel over naturally and bury his face in it, but... No, wait, wait.

"D-don't do that! I can't! I could never! And seriously, did you have to add 'like the other day'? It was bad enough already."

If someone overheard them, it would be beyond embarrassing.

Masato glanced toward the girl in the seat across from him, and she had her hand to her mouth. She was quietly giggling. She'd heard everything. He was doomed.

But then she said, "You're certainly close to your mother."

"Oh... Um, no! Not really! We're not all that close!"

"That's just not true! Ma-kun and Mommy are very close! We even went in that hot spring together!"

"Aughhhh! Why would you bring that up? She's gonna get the wrong idea...!"

"A family hot springs visit? How lovely! You really are close!"

"...Huh?"

He'd been expecting all this to creep her out, but apparently she was genuinely impressed. Thankfully. It seemed she was really pure of heart.

In his mind, she was immediately promoted to angel status.

"Oh, excuse my manners," she said. "My name is Medhi. I'm a test player... By any chance, are you all...?"

"Oh, yeah, we're..."

"Yes, we're test players! I'm Mamako. On my right is my son, Masato. The girls sleeping are Wise and Porta. So nice to meet you!"

"Um, wait, Mom, I was about to answer..."

"Oh, you're all test players?" the woman next to Medhi interrupted. "Then I'd better introduce myself, too. Pleasure meeting you. I'm Medhi's mother, and I've been calling myself Medhimama here. I do hope we'll all get along."

Neither of them seemed to mean anything by it, but Masato had now been interrupted twice in a row. Seriously.

Having introduced themselves, the two mothers quickly began chattering away about everything from life in the game to your typical...whatever the mom version of watercooler talk was.

But if they were keeping themselves distracted, that was ideal. This was his chance.

R-right... Just gotta get Medhi talking!

This was his chance to forge a bond between them. Masato fixed his gaze on the smiling angel in the seat across from him. Her face was really far too beautiful. And the swaying of the carriage was definitely making her rather ample chest bounce around like... No, no, eyes off.

Masato gritted his teeth, wrangled his courage, and was just about to speak when...

The mothers' conversation assaulted his ears.

"Oh, really? You're adventuring as a party of four? We've found two was perfectly adequate, but perhaps the more the merrier. How many quests have you completed? Ten? Twenty?"

"Oh, not at all. I believe we're maybe at five. They can be so difficult..."

"Really? I suppose so. The two of us have completed thirty, but it certainly wasn't easy."

"Thirty already? How impressive. You have my respect."

"It's hardly worth that! But, well... Out of all the test players, I think we may be the top-ranked party. At least, I feel like we are. Oh-ho-ho-ho!"

They weren't exactly talking quietly. Medhimama in particular was quite loud.

"Oh, I know! If you like, I'm happy to share the trick to making good progress in this game."

"A trick?"

"Yes. Just do exactly as I say. There's nothing difficult about it. My daughter just does whatever I tell her, and she's become ever so strong. So... Well? How about it?"

"Um... I appreciate the advice, but..."

"No need to stop there! I'm sure you want to know more."

"W-well..."

Medhimama appeared to be overpowering Mamako, who was now unobtrusively tugging at Masato's sleeve.

She seemed to want his help, but there was no way he could...

No, wait, perhaps this was his chance. Masato steeled his nerves and valiantly thrust himself into mom talk.

"Um, uh... Do you mind? I have a question."

"Oh! Your son seems interested. You see, the basis of it is..."

"N-no, not that... Um... I was wondering where the two of you were headed."

Well, he was only really interested in where *Medhi* was headed.

Medhimama seemed slightly disappointed but answered anyway.

"Our destination? Well, obviously, we're headed to the school town Mahweh. I'm planning on having Medhi attend the school there."

"Oh, really?! Same as us, then!"

This allowed the two parties—or more importantly, Masato and Medhi—to share the spotlight for a while. That was a good thing. He'd have been quite upset otherwise.

This must be destiny's hand at work.

A boy and a girl, coincidentally on the same carriage. Bound for the same place, for the same purpose.

After spending that time together, they would support each other,

growing closer and closer, until they found themselves always together...

In time, they would be unable to ignore the attraction growing between them, and those soft lips would be his to... Well, one could hope!

What else could possibly happen? I'm sure of it! Medhi and I are just beginning our story together!

He glanced her way to see an expectant smile on her face.

"Then Masato and I will be attending the same school! ...Tee-hee-hee! That should be fun! I'm really looking forward to it!"

See? See that right there? Medhi was on board! She wanted what he wanted!

It was starting! Their story was just beginning!

They spent about an hour rocking in the passenger carriage before finally reaching their destination, the town of Mahweh.

This place was also known as School Town. Like the name implied, the school building in the center of the town doubled as the town's symbol. If you went down any of the town's tight grid of roads, you'd soon see it.

The building itself was every bit as ornate as a palace, and the students who gathered would be taught all manner of things. A thought that made them all tense...

Or not, as the case may be. It didn't seem like anyone was all that tense, really.

"As I said, since parents and children are adventuring together, the parent must be the one to take the lead. It is critical that the parent issue clear instructions and continue pushing their offspring forward. Understand? It is the parent who decides how a child is raised. Only you can raise your own child."

"R-right... That much is true..."

Since long before they left the carriage, and long after they did, Medhimama had been speaking at length about her personal education theory. The endless torrent of words had left Mamako quite worn out. Porta clearly wanted to support her somehow but couldn't get a word in edgewise, and Wise was doing her best imitation of thin air.

But Masato didn't care about any of that. All he cared about...

...was that Medhi was giving him an angelic smile and talking to him.

"So you're also fifteen? First year of high school? I am, too. Wouldn't it be great if we end up in the same class?"

"Oh, uh, yeah! I agree! It would be really great!"

Did you hear that? Did you hear it? The angel spoke, and she said if they were in the same class that meant her route was open for sure! Wait, she didn't say that? Well, Masato heard it like that.

He glanced sideways, and she was standing so close their shoulders were almost touching.

This distance alone was all the answer he needed. She would definitely accept him. This was clearly a sign she was on board. He was sure of it. It was a hard-rooted conviction.

The girl next to me is my heroine. My girlfriend. I hope! You gotta hope!

But, well, that did seem to be where things were headed. It was best to be open to these possibilities.

Hoping to progress this story as fast as possible, Masato led the way through the school gates. He called out to the group wilting under Medhimama's rain of declarations. "Come on, everyone! Let's get going! Ha-ha-ha!" And led the way to reception, following signs clearly labeled APPLICANTS THIS WAY.

Now they just had to greet the official at the counter and apply.

"Hey! We're here to enroll! The paperwork of my future, if you please!"

"Understood. Then please write your name and job on this sheet."

He took the paper and filled it out. NAME: MASATO. JOB: NORMAL HERO.

Wise, Porta, and Medhi all filled their documents out as well.

"Everyone done? Then I'll turn them all in. Ma-kun's, Wise's, Porta's, and Medhi's. Five in all!"

"Thank you very much. I appreciate all your help."

"My, how polite. You certainly have flawless manners, Medhi."

"Mm. The way she does that slight bow. Her polite speech. As beautiful as she is well-bred. You can only describe her as perfect... Hey... Wait a sec..."

As much as he would have liked to continue extolling Medhi's virtues, Masato's brain had caught up with him.

Mamako had gathered up the forms and handed five of them over to the official.

Five?

"...Mom. I'm probably wrong here, but...did you fill out an application, too?"

"...Tee-hee ☆" She stuck her tongue out.

Mamako's full-body tee-hee tongue-out attack activated!

Hit full in the face by his actual mother's adorableness, Masato...

"...Gahhh..."

...takes heavy damage. He's on the brink of death.

"Whaaat?! Why did he take damage?!"

The reason was simple: because he was her son. What other outcome was there?

Mamako may have applied, but of course, they would not accept such an application. Participants were limited to children only. The official lady managed an awkward smile, quietly placed Mamako's application to one side, checked over the other applications, and placed her seal of approval on them.

But then her hands paused.

"...Oh? ... Your names... I remember them... Oh, right!"

"What's up?"

"Um... Medhi, there's no issue with you at all. We've accepted your application, so you may proceed directly to orientation. You'll receive a simple explanation of how the school works. However..."

"...What about us?"

"Masato, Wise, Porta, and Mamako, if we could have a moment of your time before orientation? There's someone who wants to speak to you."

Well, then.

Medhimama's expression grew instantly suspicious. "Um, Mamako?" she asked. "The children with you appear to have been summoned to the principal's office before they even completed enrollment. Are they…delinquents?"

"N-no! It's nothing like that at all!"

Of course it wasn't. This was…

"This again."

"Seems like it."

"I agree!"

All three of them had a pretty good idea of who wanted to see them.

And they were more or less right.

A clerk led them to the headmaster's office, where they found a coffin in the center of the room.

"A coffin? Here?"

"Any time a coffin appears in front of us, odds are it's her."

"I agree! I'm sure it's her!"

"Right… Wise, if you please?"

"Roger. I'll bring her back pronto… *Spara la magia per mirare… Rianimato!*"

The shaft of light poured down. The coffin covering the dead dissolved, and the person inside emerged.

Long black hair, excessively calm countenance, fairly attractive.

She was wearing a suit that definitely seemed like something a headmaster would wear, and the moment she was alive again, she sat up like nothing had happened and greeted them.

"Well, well, I see you've all come rushing to your dooms— To your duties. Thank you for taking the time out of your busy schedules."

"If you say the whole thing before you correct yourself, it's really not very effective."

"Allow me to cut right to the chase, then. How shall I introduce myself this time?"

"How…? Um, like…Ms. Shirassse, for example?"

"Perfect, I'll go with that. I am Shirassse. I must inforrrm you that I am the Mysterious Headmaster, Shirassse."

Right, so her name was Shirassse, then.

To be clear, her real name was Masumi Shirase. She was a government official who always showed up dead and always gave a different name and occupation, which was really obnoxious. "Were you just thinking I'm obnoxious?"

"N-no… We weren't…"

She was not to be trifled with.

"Why was I dead? …I'm sure this suspenseful development must have come as a shock to you all."

"Not so much anymore, really. You're pretty much always equally inexplicable."

"As you say, I am as inexplicable as I am inexcusable, but if you'll allow me to make excuses, I shall show you how it's done."

"Er, nobody said 'inexcusable'…"

But as obnoxious as she was, Shirassse never really listened. She walked across the room to the desk by the window.

And fused with it.

"…Uh…?"

The upper half of Shirassse's body was the same, while the lower half was now a desk. She had always been quite strange, but had she finally become half-furniture? Creepy.

But of course, that wasn't it. Masato figured it out first.

"Um, is this…a bug? One of those bugs where you can walk through an object you shouldn't be able to?"

"Indeed! And then this happens."

From her position inside the desk, Shirassse took a single step. Immediately after…

…Shirassse died. Back in the coffin. "Yeesh, a sudden-death bug." "What now? Just leave her?" "I think you'd better bring her back again." Wise cast another revival spell.

"So there you have it. Thoughts?"

"We get it. You were dead because of that bug. This school was hastily slapped together and has bugs everywhere."

"I'm so pleased you understand... Now that we have solved the bug masquerading as a locked-room murder trick, let us get down to business. If you would?"

Shirassse led the party to the reception area, took a seat herself, and began to explain.

"Let's begin. I'd like to thank you for answering the call for students. As far as the school itself goes, creation of the headmaster character wasn't completed in time, so someone said, 'Can you fill in?' and here I am."

"Isn't that so often the way? We're with you."

"The school's name is officially Gioco Accademia. The school was created to silence a stream of complaints from a certain guardian to the effect of 'This may be a game, but as long as children live here, it makes no sense that there isn't a school.' To that end, it was rather hastily put together."

"Maybe we don't need to know that part."

"Gioco Accademia allows you to earn SP by taking part in classes and getting good grades. And these points can be exchanged for special power-up items. If we don't offer some benefit, we'd never get any students, so..."

"Yes! I want that amazing item!"

"Hee-hee," Mamako said. "Looks like someone took the bait!"

"Bait it may be," Shirassse admitted. "But improving yourselves is hardly a bad thing. If it makes you take the classes seriously, then our goals align. But that's all there really is to say about the school itself. Any questions?"

Masato's hand shot up.

"Just one... The flyer posted at the Adventurers Guild had a note written on it that seemed aimed rather specifically at us."

"You noticed that? Well done. It was well worth personally visiting each guild branch to write that note in so I could convince you to come here."

"I figured as much. You sure got us hook, line, and sinker. So…did you have some job for us? Beyond just attending the school, I mean?"

"Oh! I know!" Wise said, raising her hand. "You want us to help with the bugs, right? You've got too many bugs like that one you just showed us!"

Shirassse shook her head. *Bzzt.*

"Operations is forever short staffed, so certainly assistance with debugging would be welcomed. And you have a duty to resolve issues that are beyond management's resources, so it's only natural you'd assume as much. However…"

"No, wait, I don't think that's actually our duty or anything…"

"It is in my mind," she said firmly.

"You can't just decide that!"

"But I will be handling the debugging. You can just do what comes naturally to you. You seem to have already established a connection without us doing anything. I leave it all in your capable hands."

"Um, what's that supposed to mean?"

"That would be telling!"

Shirassse gave a rare smile. But she seemed disinclined to inforrrm them of what that smile meant.

"With that said, we welcome your participation in this school with open arms. Enjoy your time here, engaging in cheap heroic clichés like the desire to become stronger, lusting after those power-up items, helping out your friends, and tripping them at the last minute because this is, after all, a competition."

"You make everything sound so unpleasant. How do you always manage that?"

What she said hit uncomfortably close to home, which made it all the worse.

But it wasn't all bad!

School life… Hopefully Medhi and I are in the same class.

Masato was so excited about that, he'd almost forgotten the original goal.

And thus, their time at the Gioco Accademia adventurer training school began.

Chapter 2 School Is Filled with Thrills! ...Sounds Good, but It's Mostly Exhausting.

Their time at school would last a single week. Masato's party took rooms at the inn in town and would have to trudge into school each day. Here, they were in a game, doing the same thing they'd do in the real world. A depressing thought, but those were the breaks.

The rooms at the inn were, as always, built for two. The group paired off just as they always did, so Masato and Wise were sharing a room.

And just like usual, she cast Morte on him in the evening, and he spent the night resting in peace inside a coffin.

"What the...? It's still dark..."

That morning, he woke up and emerged from his coffin to find himself surrounded by darkness.

Masato couldn't see a thing. It was like a dark mist before his eyes.

"Um, Wise... What's happening to me? Please explain."

"When I revived you, I also cast a Blind effect on you. You know, the one that makes it easy for your attacks to miss? Standard stuff."

"Aha. That explains it."

It definitely severely limited Masato's ability to act. He reached out, trying to grab anything, but kept missing. It was extremely frustrating.

"Why would you do this? Can you please stop? I think it's a little much."

"I'm merely protecting my privacy. Since you're sleeping in the same room as me, there's always a risk of you seeing me naked somehow. But if I make it impossible for you to see, there's no risk of that. And I don't have to punish you. See?"

"Well... I suppose it's better than pointlessly pissing you off and getting my eyes literally poked out, but..."

"Now that we're in agreement, hurry up and get ready. Can't be late for our first day."

"I agree with you there, but...how am I supposed to get ready like this? I can wait until you're ready, but please cancel the spell."

He really couldn't see anything. He took a single step and stubbed a toe—"Ow!"—and almost fell over. He reached out a hand to catch himself.

"Whoops..." His hand touched something squishy. Squishy and soft. Spongy and springy.

Uh... Is this...?!

It couldn't be. Had Masato seriously landed a critical touch?!

But hang on. Whatever Masato was touching was quite large. So large he couldn't even get his whole hand around it. Wise wasn't exactly equipped with anything so bountiful...

That was when it hit him.

"Goodness, Ma-kun! Is that what you want for breakfast? Hee-hee."

"...Eep..."

He knew that voice. All too well. It was like she was right there.

Then that meant the soft something he was now cupping belonged to *her*...

No, wait. Wait, wait, wait. Waitwaitwaitwaitwaitwaitwaitwait waitwaitwait!!

"Hey, Masato. I'm done getting ready, so want me to restore your sight now? Heh. Heh. Heh."

"N-noooooooooooooooooooooooooooooooooooooooooo!!!"

He refused to acknowledge this reality! He turned on his heel and ran for it. "Ah, Ma-kun! Not that way!" "Have a nice trip!" "Huh...?" One second he was running, the next second there was nothing underfoot.

Masato fell out the window. Self-punishment: complete.

When they entered the inn dining room, the smell of miso soup filled the air. Japanese-style breakfast was laid out on the table. Porta was there, waiting.

"I thought I heard a loud crash, like something falling! I wonder what it was?"

"Hee-hee. That was Ma-kun."

"*Pfft.* You see…"

"Nothing happened! Nothing at all! There was nothing weird! Right, Mom?! You need more rice? Wise, have some more soup! I'll help fetch them! Ask me for anything! Ha-ha-ha!"

Masato eagerly busied himself helping, hoping to seal their lips. He did NOT want Porta knowing about any of that. He wanted to remain a cool older brother to her forever, and this made him desperate.

After a lively breakfast…

"Thanks for the food! …Right then, we'd better getting going… right away!"

Masato was looking forward to school. He wanted to be there already. Never in his life had he wanted to be at school so much.

If he was at school, he was sure…

"Yeesh, what's gotten into him? Look at his face! He's gone full creepy 'a destined encounter awaits me'! What an idiot."

"I'm not an idiot! Maybe I did look a little like that, but I'm not wrong! I think destiny really is waiting for me!"

"U-um… Masato! Wise! Let's stop fighting and go to school. I really want to get there myself!"

"Mm, exactly. Right you are, Porta. We can't be wasting time on idle chatter. Now, the three of us are off to school, but…"

Masato did feel a little guilty about Mamako.

Three of them were going to school. Mamako was not. So she'd be left behind at the inn, all on her own.

Mamako enjoyed spending time with him more than anything, but now they were forced to spend time apart. That could be really hard on her…

And that wasn't his only worry.

…*She won't, like…show up at school, will she?*

That was maybe his greatest fear. It was Mamako, after all.

Since they'd entered the game, Mamako had become extremely proactive.

And she'd received mom-only support blessings that made things you'd think were impossible rather easy for her to accomplish.

The woman herself did not appear to be paying their conversation any attention. She was calmly sipping at her cup of tea. But that behavior, in and of itself, seemed highly suspicious...

"...Um, Mom?"

"Hee-hee. Don't worry. I've been a housewife all this time. I spent all day at home alone! I know how to hold down the fort. Don't you worry about me."

"Sure, that's true, but...are you really just gonna wait for us to get back? Are you just gonna behave yourself alone? You won't find some excuse to show up at school, right?"

He wanted this made very clear.

Mamako took another sip of tea and sighed.

"...Phew. What lovely tea," she said, satisfied.

"Quit looking so satisfied and answer me! You're gonna behave yourself, right? You're not gonna butt in where you're not supposed to?"

"Oh, look, Ma-kun! It's almost time! You'd better hurry or you'll be late."

"Seriously, answer the questions! Whatever you do, don't come to school..."

"Oh, that's right. Mommy made lunches for everyone! They're in Porta's bag, so make sure to eat them when the time comes, okay?"

Mamako was clearly being evasive. She refused to answer the questions. In which case...

"Porta, question. How many lunches did she give you?"

"Huh?! ...U-um... Well..."

Porta jumped, then froze, her eyes wide as saucers, sweat pouring down her face. Like her name was now Pourta. Ha-ha. Wait, this was no time for puns.

Porta had definitely been handed four lunches. He knew it. Mamako had included one for herself.

Which meant...

"...Mom."

"Hee-hee. I sure do love tea!"

"Answer! The! Questions! Promise you won't come! You can't come! Say you won't come!"

Mamako met Masato's interrogation with a smile, pretending to sip from a long-empty teacup.

"...She's coming... She's definitely coming... Mom's gonna come..."

"What are you muttering about now, creep?"

"Don't call me a creep! I'm seriously worried here! If Mom worms her way into class pretending to be a student, lord knows what'll happen!"

"I think Mama could be a student! Mama's super young!"

"That's exactly why I'm so worried... I'm really scared she'll blend in like she belongs there..."

The first day of school was scary for anybody, but Masato was being crushed by anxiety quite removed from the norm. Oh well.

They arrived at the adventurer training school, Gioco Accademia.

Masato alone was preoccupied with looking over his shoulder as they stepped onto the beautiful school grounds. They first stopped by the front desk they'd visited the day before, and the same reception lady greeted them with a smile.

"Wait right here until your teacher comes to get you," she said.

So they waited. Their teacher arrived soon enough.

Striding down the hall came a male teacher, burly body wrapped in academic garb, his bellow echoing like a starting pistol.

"Hey! You guys must be the students starting today! Masato the Hero, Wise the Sage, Porta the Traveling Merchant! All present and accounted for?"

"Oh yes! That's us!"

"Right, right! Welcome! I'm your teacher, Mr. Burly! Good to meet you!"

"P-pleasure... Like body, like name, I guess... Sorry, I hate to point this out, but that really is a lazy name..."

"Bwa-ha-ha! Well, I am an NPC! I dunno if it was the writer or the artist, but one of them was definitely too lazy to bother coming up with a decent name, so they just called me as they saw me! Such sloppy work, honestly!"

"Oh, I see… Being an NPC must be tough…"

The NPC teacher led them to the classroom, griping about management to the limits of his artificial intelligence the whole way. The hall was a luxurious affair, with plush carpeting.

Mr. Burly seemed to be quite an easygoing teacher. His friendly demeanor belied his rough-hewn exterior.

"If you've got any questions, ask away! I can handle any of them! They've programmed the entire text of the school-related FAQ within me!"

An FAQ was a list of frequently asked questions. Very useful when at a loss.

"Wow, just like a real NPC. That sounds handy. So I was wondering… Are we being treated like transfer students?"

"Yes. All the test players transfer in and undergo a special accelerated course. That allows you to experience all the school has to offer within a week, and the classes are a special curriculum designed for all ages, so the three of you are in the same class."

"Oh, that's great! Good news, Porta! You're in the same class as us!"

"Yes! Ooooh! I'm so very, very happy!"

"And in a week's time, we'll all graduate with awesome items! A flawless life plan!"

"Oh, by the way, the other students are supposed to be enrolled in a standard three-year course. Three years means, honestly, they'll be students until this game ends. After all, they're NPCs made to fill out the student body! Like myself, they're trapped here until it all comes crashing down! Bwa-ha-ha! …So anyway, try to be nice to the poor kids who'll never actually graduate."

""""…I don't think I'll ever be able to look my classmates in the eye…""""

This place was dark. An academic sweatshop. The student NPC was not allowed any hopes or dreams…only pity.

Just as the emotional roller coaster reached its lowest point, they arrived at their classroom. "Come on in when I call your names," Mr. Burly said. He went in, and they waited in the hall. A bit nervous.

Then their moment arrived.

"Beloved students!" Mr. Burly bellowed. "Today we have several new friends transferring in! Let me introduce you all! Come on in!"

Feeling tense, Masato's party filed in.

The classroom interior was fairly typical. The desks and chairs themselves were quite fancy and arranged in perfectly neat rows.

The students in the seats were wearing uniforms—stiff-collared military-style attire for the boys, and sailor uniforms for the girls. There were around twenty of them in all.

The party blinked a little at seeing such standard-issue uniforms inside a video game fantasy school, but...that was hardly the biggest problem.

Every face staring up at them was made with ASCII art. Where eyes and mouths should be were letters and symbols. Seriously. What the hell.

"Urgh... I guess we can still register their emotions somehow, but there's no way to tell them apart..."

"That's hardly the real problem here! This is ridiculous! I mean, there's sloppy, and then there's just downright unprofessional!"

"Whoever was in charge of making NPCs must have been really short on time! This is so shocking!"

The unnervingly slapdash faces ensured they would literally never look a classmate in the eye.

Even so, they had to introduce themselves. They lined up before the blackboard and said their piece.

"Um... H-hi. I'm Masato. Technically a hero."

"'Sup, I'm Wise. I'm a Sage. Nice to meetcha."

"I-I'm Porta! I'm a Traveling Merchant! Thank you very much!"

There was a silence, then a sudden eruption of applause.

"Whoa! All three of you are so original! They broke the molds after you! Nothing like us mass-produced people!"

"The guy's pretty normal-looking, but both girls are super cute! Can I ask a question? Do either of you have boyfriends? If not, would you go out with me?"

"Hey! Boys! That's enough of that! I know that's just what you were programmed to say, but that doesn't make it any less weird!"

"Shut up, Class President! Quit making that angry emoticon face; it's so annoying!"

"Don't be rude! Better than having a face made entirely of horizontal lines like yours!"

Okay. Well, at least someone gave them voices. The words that accompanied those voices were all kinds of problematic, and their faces were still all ASCII. But at least it seemed like their classmates were happy to see them.

Mr. Burly waited for the commotion to subside and then clapped his hands, calling for silence.

"All right, be nice to the new kids. You three can sit anywhere you like."

"R-right," Masato said, glancing around. There was a cluster of empty seats toward the back. "Well… Over there is fine, I guess."

Masato took a seat at random, with Wise on his right and Porta behind him.

"Well, with the three new students… Hmm? Three?" Mr. Burly frowned. "One…two…three…" He counted them again, his scowl deepening.

"Something wrong?"

"Oh, um… It's a little late, but I could swear there were four new students today… I'm pretty sure we were expecting four…"

"Then there's still one coming? …Wait… That can't mean…?!"

A face flitted across Masato's mind; it looked young enough that its owner could conceivably claim to be a student, and a wave of despair washed over him.

But then he heard footsteps coming down the hall. Someone clearly in a hurry. They stopped outside the door.

Could it be? No, it definitely was! She was here!

"Wha…? Seriously?! What the hell, Mom?!"

He had to prevent this at all costs! Masato dashed over to the door and attempted to put his shoulder against it...but the door was already open.

And standing there was a girl with blue hair, in pure-white robes.

"Huh? 'M-Mom'?" she said.

"Erm... Wait... You're not Mom... Medhi?"

Yep. Definitely Medhi. His destined partner whom he'd met only yesterday. Masato's prospective heroine. He'd know her angelic face anywhere.

Masato and Medhi stared into each other's eyes, surprised, until Wise yelled, "Um, Hero Masato? Earth to Masato? Is there something wrong with your eyes or do all women look like your beloved mommy now?"

"H-hey! That's not what I..."

The classmates all burst out laughing.

Masato's only salvation was that it wasn't a nasty, mean laugh, but even so, he wasn't exactly feeling great. More like he wanted to die. Shortly after killing Wise.

Also, Mr. Burly was laughing harder than anyone, so he definitely wanted to punch him. Not that he actually would.

"Bwa-ha-ha! Then can your surprisingly young mother introduce herself?"

"Oh, yes! I'm Medhi! I'm a Cleric! ...Um, also... I'm not actually Masato's mother, so..."

Medhi turned toward Masato and bowed politely. Too politely.

"I'm sorry to dash your hopes like that. I apologize. From the bottom of my heart."

"Please don't do that. I'm the one who should be apologizing..."

There were few things more painful than a polite apology. Masato was ready to plant his face on the floor.

Then.

"Oh, but I am glad!"

"Huh...? About what...?"

"I'm so glad we're both in the same class... Perhaps this is destiny? Oh, I can't believe I just said that. Tee-hee-hee!"

Medhi gave him a smile that looked genuinely happy and a little embarrassed.

I agreeeeeeeeeeeeeeeeeeeeeeeeeeee, Masato nearly yelled, but she was right there, so he managed to control himself. He had to keep his cool. On the surface anyway.

The morning homeroom-ish period wrapped up, and there was a break before the first actual class of the day began.

But there was no rest for the transfer students. They had to deal with swarms of friendly classmates. It was the duty of any transfer student.

"Masato! If there's anything you don't understand about school, just ask! Although…the facilities are all still trial versions, so we can't really explain much about them. Instead, you'll have to ask about us! We'll answer everything!"

"Ask me, too! I can tell you every name in my family tree going back fifteen generations!"

"I can give you a month-by-month account of the one hundred eighty months it took me to turn fifteen!"

"Oh, uh, w-wow… They may have scrimped on your visuals, but they sure did buckle down on your backgrounds…"

"Yep! Our histories are the most developed things about us! Hilarious, right? Ah-ha-ha!"

"I guess they just like working on that stuff! A shame it's so useless! Ah-ha-ha!"

"But that's the only thing we can really take pride in! Sad, right? Ah-ha-ha!"

"You're all…living the best lives you can…"

The NPC classmates' open, cheery dispositions were like freshly chopped onions. Masato found himself shedding tears on their behalf.

It didn't take all that long for each to greet him, after which his stalwart classmates politely went back to their seats.

At last, he had a minute to rest. He glanced to one side, where

Wise and Porta were still buried in questions, and leaned back in his seat.

He allowed himself a single, long sigh and decided that was rest enough.

...All right! Here goes nothing!

Inside, he was pumping himself up, but on the outside, he maintained his cool. Masato stole a quick glance to his left.

Where Medhi sat.

She had chosen that seat without making a show of it. She had voluntarily chosen to sit next to Masato. This was her choice. She was here because she wanted a relationship with him. He was sure of it.

Perhaps Medhi was a little too beautiful for them—the other classmates weren't approaching her at all. It was just her and Masato, the two of them. This was his chance. If he didn't seize it, he was hardly worth calling a man!

He was going for it—casually, not showing how much he was stressing this.

"Ha-hay, um… *Cough, cough*… H-hey, Medhi? Got a sec?"

"Yes? What is it?"

Masato had blown it entirely, but Medhi just smiled gently, answering easily.

The way she tucked her hair behind her ear was almost too much for Masato. *Calm down. Just make conversation.*

"Um, I don't really have anything in particular; I just thought this would be a good chance to talk. I mean…we didn't really get to talk much yesterday."

"That's true! I wanted to speak to you more, too. I'm very glad you reached out to me."

Did you hear that?! He wasn't mishearing this! A girl was actually happy he'd spoken to her!

He could search every world out there and there would be only a handful like her! He had no choice but to love her with every fiber of his being. "Uh-oh, I'm starting to tear up…" "M-Masato? What's wrong?" He just wanted to quietly savor this emotion, but…

He had to keep talking.

Um... S-so, what do we talk about?

He'd made a start at least but had failed to think of an actual topic. Things were certainly headed the right direction, but this could be a real stumbling block...

Just then, Mr. Burly's voice echoed from the hall.

"M-ma'am! Wait just a minute! You can't just drop in for an unannounced classroom inspection!"

He seemed to be trying his hardest to stop someone. Judging from the *ma'am*, this was a grown woman. Someone's mother?

Masato froze. Was it really her this time? Apparently not. The voice he heard next was not Mamako's.

"Fear not. I am merely here to check on my daughter, not watch the class. In my opinion, school is not a place to learn but a means to determine which students rise to the top and which do not. The content of the classes is irrelevant. I merely wish to ascertain all the ways in which my daughter is the best."

With that haughty spiel, Medhi's mother, Medhimama, stepped into the room, her gold nouveau riche robes gleaming. There was no mistaking her.

Medhimama pushed past Mr. Burly, glanced around the room, located Medhi, and came directly over to her. As she approached, her gaze locked onto Masato.

"Oh, we met you yesterday... Masato, was it? Good morning."

"Y-yeah. Hi. Good morning."

"If Medhi is this close to you, I assume you are getting along. That's nice. But...I feel you're a little too close."

"Huh? R-really? ...I don't think we are, but..."

"No, much too close. I do not approve. Which means... Come, Medhi. Move over one seat."

"Y-yes, Mother."

Once Medhi moved, Medhimama sat down in the seat between her and Masato, as if she belonged there. And if that wasn't bad enough...

"Should you be entertaining any thoughts about inviting Medhi to your party or any relationship above and beyond that, Masato, I ask that you discuss it with me first. I will conduct a thorough interview. We'll discuss particulars once that is concluded."

"Eep... A mom interview..."

For Masato and Medhi to get any closer, he'd have to do one of those...a mandatory mom interview, where he'd be evaluated by whatever biased and arbitrary standards she had, failed for saying things anyone else would consider totally acceptable.

Here destiny had brought the two of them together, yet an impregnable wall of motherhood sprang up between them. There was no way he'd be able to easily speak to her again.

"Now then, Masato, sit down. It's time for class to start."

"...Right..."

His own mom was bad enough, but being tormented by someone else's? Was this what fate held in store for all heroes, or just Masato in particular?

A hero who had passed through any number of worlds and defeated any number of powerful enemies would be dashed against the cliffs of despair in Masato's shoes. Tears would flow. They'd cry themselves to sleep at night.

Class was off to a great start.

First period.

"Okay, class! Picking up from where we left off yesterday...is not what I'm doing, since we have transfer students and have changed up the entire curriculum for their benefit! NPCs have no right of refusal in their operational settings, so the special curriculum's first period will be..."

"No need for the long-winded preamble. Move along to the actual lesson."

"R-right..."

Mr. Burly managed to avoid wilting under Medhimama's piercing glare, but he did break into a cold sweat. Hang in there, Mr. Burly!

"Th-then let's get started. Eyes up!"

Mr. Burly began writing on the blackboard.

$\{(Level \div 2 + 2) \times Skill\ Power \times Attacker\ STR\ stat \div Defender\ DEF\ stat \div 50 + 2\}$

A fairly complex formula.

"Erm, this is the formula for how damage is calculated in battle. Everything after the decimal is discarded. So the problem: If a level 50 hero with an STR of 125 uses Divine Slash with a power of 255 on a demon lord with a DEF of 100, how much damage will they do? If you get this right, you'll receive 10 SP."

"Whoa, that much right off the bat?"

"Bwa-ha-ha! Good reaction, Hero Masato! You'll receive the points instantly, so rake them in! But the fastest answer wins. Raise your hand as soon as you've figured it out!"

Normally you could only get a few SP each time you leveled up. Getting ten at once? They had to take this seriously.

But the problem was a little too tricky. "*Tch...* Gotta work it out ourselves, huh?" There were no calculators. Masato scribbled the problem down using the pen and paper on his desk and started working through the calculations...

But.

"Got it!" Medhi said, her hand raised. Less than ten seconds had passed.

"Oh, that was fast. Cleric Medhi, what is the answer?"

"174 damage."

"Mm, correct! Ten points to the Cleric!"

Medhi got it right. A buzz went around the class, followed by a round of applause.

Despite the shower of praise, Medhi showed no signs of letting her achievement go to her head. She simply politely bowed her head. Even this was beautiful but difficult to see past Medhimama, who leaned forward, saying, "Heh-heh-heh. She is my daughter, so naturally she's quite extraordinary!" Geez, lady.

When Medhi sat down, Mr. Burly picked up his chalk again.

"Right, next problem. This is a tricky one!"

Something more difficult than that formula? Masato and the other students faced forward, bracing themselves.

The following was written on the board:

The hero used Divine Slash. But the Demon Lord took no damage.

"Now, what does this mean? If you can't figure it out, you'll never beat the Demon Lord. It'll attack you, and you'll lose. Hurry up now—answer! Ten SP to whoever gets it right."

How could he answer this out of the blue? No, he had to at least try. Otherwise, he'd never get any points. Masato racked his brain.

It's soaking the damage… Does it have some damage nullification effect?

Masato had fought enemies like that before, so that answer popped into his head quickly. He wasn't sure if it was right or not, but sometimes the shotgun approach was best. He'd better at least answer.

Masato raised his hand…or at least, he tried.

For some reason, he couldn't do it.

"…Huh?"

He was trying to raise his hand, but it just wouldn't budge. Confused, he looked down at it.

The head of a bejeweled staff was pressing firmly on his wrist.

Medhimama was holding that staff with one hand and had her other hand raised.

"Mr. Burly, if I may?"

"Hm? …Um, no, this class is for the children. We ask that parents and guardians please refrain from—"

"Naturally, it will be my daughter answering, not myself… Well, Medhi? The correct answer, please."

"Yes, Mother… I believe the Demon Lord has cast an illusion, and its real body is hidden somewhere else."

"There you have it. What do you say, Mr. Burly?"

"Uh, yeah, that's right. So ten points to the Cleric! Congratulations!"

"Thank—"

"Oh-ho-ho! The only possible outcome!"

Ding-ding-ding! There was a pleasant sound effect, and Medhi's

SP increased. Medhimama seemed much happier about this than the one who actually earned the points, but that aside...

Masato's hand was still pinned down.

"Um, Medhimama...?"

"Yes, Masato, what is it? ...Goodness me! My staff just happens to have fallen coincidentally in your direction and accidentally pinned your hand down!" Medhimama said, leaning her staff against her desk. She seemed genuinely apologetic. "Gosh, I'm so sorry! I never noticed. I can't apologize enough."

"Oh, um... Well, if it wasn't intentional..."

He'd definitely thought it was a conscious effort with a lot of force behind it, so he wasn't entirely convinced...but his answer was wrong anyway, so he'd been spared looking the fool in front of Medhi. He let it pass.

The class came first. He had to score some points next time.

"Next problem. The hero attacks! But the Demon Lord takes no damage. This sudden twist shocks the hero. And the Demon Lord says... What does he say?"

"Huh? What on...?"

"I wrote this problem myself! If I like your answer, ten points!"

"What the heck? Is that appropriate for this class?"

But if he could get points for it, it was worth a shot. Whoever spoke first won. "Argh, let's just do it!" Masato tried to raise his hand...but before he could...

"Yes! Yes, yes, yes, yes! I thought of something! Me!"

Masato looked to his right. Wise had her hand up and was frantically trying to draw the teacher's attention. He hadn't even called on her yet, but she was on her feet and ready to answer.

Or so he thought.

"The answer is... H-huh? Huhhh? Huhhhhhhh? Meep? Uh-heh-heh-heh-heh?!"

Wise suddenly began acting incredibly stupid, grinning like an idiot. She even started dancing. This was much too bizarre. Masato had never seen her acting this silly. Had she lost her mind?

"What's gotten into her? Did she finally snap?"

"Wise is Confused! I'll give her a recovery item!" Behind her, Porta sprang to the rescue. "Wise, here!"

"Take it, shake it, toss it!" She tossed it. "Don't throw thaaaat!!" Confused Wise was even more of a handful than usual. Maybe they should just knock her out.

Meanwhile, Medhimama raised her hand.

"There seems to be a great deal of commotion, but in the meantime, my daughter will answer."

"R-right... Cleric Medhi, what did the Demon Lord say to the hero when his attack missed?"

"Heh-heh-heh! Your attacks are useless against me, puny hewo! ...Ah..."

She'd blown the last word. Medhi had been so into her cackling performance as the hero she'd totally turned the *r* into a *w*. "...Uggghhh..." She flushed bright red, looking about ready to catch fire. It was adorable.

"Bwa-ha-ha! Not bad, not bad! Maybe a little cliché, but messing up when you least expect it was pretty great! Ten points to the Cleric!"

"Th-thank you... Ugh... That was so embarrassing."

"Of course she got it right! That is my daughter! She is flawless! Ohhh-ho-ho-ho!"

Medhi walked away with the points again. And once more, Medhimama seemed far happier about it than the girl herself. Watching her gloat was no fun at all, so Masato ignored her.

Porta had finally managed to cure Wise's status ailment. She came over to Masato and whispered, "Masato, listen... About Wise..."

"You don't say? That was the real her?! I knew it!"

"N-no! That's not... That's not what I mean!"

"Sorry, sorry, I'm kidding... You're talking about how she got that status ailment?"

Porta nodded gravely.

Wise had extremely low resistance to status ailments. Her resistance stat was almost certainly a big ol' zero. With her magic sealed, she made for the worst Sage ever, without fail. And this time, she'd wound up **Confused**.

And they had a pretty good idea how.

This is sabotage… She's trying to get her daughter more points.

Just as she'd physically restrained Masato.

It was obvious who the culprit was…but…

"I think that staff's behind it, but… Mmm… H-huh? I'm… getting…so sleepy… *Yawn… Zzz…*"

Porta swayed adorably; then her cheek hit the desk, and she was fast asleep. "Uh, Porta? What the…?!" Masato called, shaking her, and taking full advantage of this opportunity to rub the hell out of her cheeks. She didn't wake up. They were as soft as they looked.

She looked so content as she slept that he wanted to just sit and watch her forever, but now was clearly not the time.

Porta wasn't the only one asleep. Wise had collapsed on her desk as well, and so had the NPC students.

Only Masato, Medhimama, Medhi herself, and Mr. Burly were still conscious.

"Mm? What's all this? So many of you are nodding off… Oh well. Education is what you make of it! You may do as you please. Next problem! …Having realized he can't attack the Demon Lord directly, the hero pleads with the Demon Lord, suggesting they settle their differences by other means…"

Mr. Burly was clearly not going to do anything about this state of affairs. He was just an NPC. Perhaps he wasn't programmed to handle emergencies.

Masato had to do something. He was the only one who could.

"…I think this is going a bit too far," he said, not looking at her, speaking to the room at large but making his displeasure clear.

He heard a soft chuckle next to him.

"Heh-heh-heh. I don't know what you mean… You seem like a very serious student, Masato. Aren't you at all sleepy?"

"My armor comes with status ailment resistance. It isn't perfect, but I'm not about to be done in by your cheap tricks."

"You have resistance to it? My, my, how cunning. I find that quite aggravating… But if your resistance isn't perfect, then you can only block a certain percentage of the effects, correct? In that case, I simply have to up the casting count."

Medhimama reached for the staff at her side and touched it. That was it. That was all she did.

But instantly, Masato's body felt extremely heavy. Like his body was drifting away from him, his mind growing blurry, his eyelids drooping.

"Ungh... Are you, serious? ...So sleepy..."

"Have a nice nap. Ohhh-ho-ho-ho! Now no one is in her way! My daughter will answer every problem, obtain all the points, and achieve the highest results!"

"Dammit... You're the worst..."

"Oh, come now. There's no need for that. I'm the best mother!"

"...Yeah, right... In what way...?"

"For my daughter's sake, sometimes it is necessary to kick others aside. No need to consider the ethics of it! It is all for her benefit. That is what any mother should think. Anything done for the sake of my daughter is excusable. Naturally. That's simply how it is."

Medhimama spoke with utter certainty.

Her child was all that mattered. Perhaps he could understand her line of thinking up to a certain point.

But even then, he wasn't about to agree with her. He wasn't ready to sit there and let her kick the stool out from under him.

It really pissed him off. So aggravating...

"...*Sigh*... What a pain in the..."

That quiet whisper wasn't Masato.

So who was it? But before he could look around to see, Masato was fast asleep.

When Masato's party woke up, the first period was already over. They were on break.

The NPC students were all saying things like, "Crap, I fell asleep!"

"Me too!" They laughed like they'd just nodded off in a boring class.

Meanwhile, Masato's group was extremely disgruntled. Wise, who wanted that item more than anything, was especially livid.

"Ugh! What's her problem?! I've never been so angry in my entire life! ...Hey, Masato! What's going on here?! I'm not gonna let her get away with this! Hell no!"

"Dunno why you're yelling at me. You should be yelling at the real culprit... But since she's left her seat, I guess you can't..."

Medhimama had gone off somewhere. The bathroom, perhaps? It seemed rude to pry, so he abandoned that line of thought.

Wise wasn't letting it go.

"Masato! Someone needs to get a piece of my mind, and you'll do in a pinch! You're good at being a punching bag anyway!"

"Uh, I wouldn't exactly call that a skill of mine. I'm not here for you to take your frustrations out on!"

"I'll take them out on whoever I like! Arrghh! Just stand there and let me punch you!"

"No way! Knock it off! That's it, you're going in a headlock!"

When Wise took a wild swing at him, Masato wheeled around behind her and slipped his arm around her head.

"Ow, ow, ow!! H-hey! You can't do this to a girl!"

"Headlocks are gender neutral."

Securing her temples was proof of friendship.

Once Wise had calmed down, Masato and Porta held a quick strategy session.

"What I don't get is how she did it... She didn't chant a spell at all, yet she can cause Confusion and Sleep? That's gotta be the power of her equipment... Hey, Porta, is there anything you can tell us about Medhimama's staff?"

"Yes! I did sneakily appraise her staff, and it allows the wielder to use any magic they know at no MP cost! She can use magic without chanting a spell at all!"

"Magic with no MP or cast time? That's crazy OP."

"Yes! Crazy! But items like that usually have a downside, in that the spell that goes off is random. I don't think she should be able to choose the effect it casts…"

"Yet, Medhimama clearly can. Let's assume that staff is mom-only cheat gear. That would at least explain it…but the fact that it worked on you as well is a bit much."

"Yes! I was surprised! I'm registered as a noncombatant, so it shouldn't have!"

"Seems like they really programmed it badly. And Medhimama's not exactly gonna stop using it. We're gonna have to do something to counter it somehow… Hmm…"

"What should we do? Hmm…"

Masato and Porta trailed off in thought.

"Oh! I have an idea! You know what this calls for? An eye for an eye!"

The object in Masato's arms started squawking again, so he tightened the headlock to shut her up. *Squeeeeeeeze.*

Like he was trying to crack Wise's skull.

"Ow, ow, ow! …Just kidding! Gotcha!" "Ouch!"

Wise had suddenly jumped, headbutting Masato right in the chin and freeing herself from his grasp.

"Listen to me for once! This is a good idea, I swear! This'll definitely let us beat that old bat!"

"Old bat? Of all the phrases… Besides, I really don't have time for your dumb ideas right now…"

"It's not dumb! This situation calls for…Mamako!"

"Yes! I agree! Mama won't lose!"

"Argh… That's what I was afraid of."

An eye for an eye. A mom for a mom. It did make sense.

Mamako was undoubtedly ridiculously powerful in every conceivable way. If you needed someone to stand up to Medhimama, you couldn't ask for anyone better than Mamako. She was totally up to the task.

But even so…

"Um, hang on. Can we consider my feelings here?"

"Who cares about your feelings?"

"I do... This is a school, y'know. A place for kids. Having your mom show up here to bail you out? You might as well be dead."

"Huh?" Wise scoffed. "Oh please, it ain't that bad."

"If my mommy showed up here, I'd be really happy!" Porta said, hopping up and down. "So, so happy! I'd jump for joy!" She was jumping at the very thought.

"Okay, maybe that's just one difference between boys and girls, and, Porta, you're still pretty little, so maybe you don't get it yet... But like, seriously, no. I just can't do that."

"Hmm... Hey, Porta, you following him?"

"Um... Not really, no..."

"You don't need to get it. Just...pretend we never discussed this. Don't want that whole 'speak of the devil' thing happening, after all. Let's just move on. Next idea."

But just as Masato forced the topic closed...

A chime echoed over the PA system.

"Attention, all students. Hero Masato, Hero Masato. Your heroine awaits. Please come to the headmaster's office immediately."

It was a woman's voice. Somewhat muffled, like she was holding her nose.

Wise and Porta frowned.

"Um... Didn't that sound like Shirassse?"

"Yes! She's trying to disguise her voice, but I think it's her."

Shirassse was clearly not fooling either of them.

But Masato wasn't on the same page. Heck, he wasn't even in the same room as them.

"My heroine is waiting for me?! ...*Gasp!* You mean Medhi?! ...Okay! I'll be right there! Here I coooooooooooooooooooooooooooooome!"

Masato had gone flying out of the classroom.

"She's waiting! My heroine is waiting for me!" he yelled, racing down the hall. "Oh! Wait, time-out!" He burst into the men's room, fixed his hair in the mirror, and was off again. At speeds that totally messed his hair up again. Bound for the meeting of destiny in the headmaster's office.

And when Masato got there, his eyes beheld a huggable figure, an alluringly short skirt, a girl in a sailor uniform, her back to him...

Huh? Sailor uniform?

W-wait... If she's wearing the uniform...is she a normal student? Not Medhi?

The outfit was one thing, but the hair color and style were all wrong. This girl's hair was chestnut and fell in gentle waves. Nothing like Medhi's.

But there was still a chance she was a heroine. It was totally possible that a secondary heroine would show up to be the first heroine's rival. That sort of thing happened all the time.

M-man... I'm getting nervous...

It was time to face her. Masato took a deep breath, stepped forward, and spoke.

"U-um... Are you my heroine?"

She turned around. It was...

"Yes, it's me, Ma-kun!"

Mamako.

Masato sighed.

"I knew it. I had a feeling that's what it would be."

"O-oh? Ma-kun, you're awfully calm. I thought you'd be so mad when you saw me here."

"Ha-ha-ha. Hardly. I'm not about to start yelling 'You've gotta be kidding!' or 'You're breaking my heaaaaart!' I'm not the kind of kid who loses it over something like this. You ought to trust your son a little more, you know."

He even kept a smile on his lips.

But the fists buried deep in his pockets were clenched so tight they turned white. All his emotions concentrated there. His rage gauge at max. He could use an ultra-super-ultimate attack on a dime.

But on the surface, he stayed calm. He wasn't a dumb kid.

"How about you start by explaining the outfit?"

"This? Well, Shirassse sent it to me. She said I might as well consider it a sort of memento. The junior high I went to had sailor uniforms, so it really takes me back, and I just had to try it on. Well? Does it look good?"

Mamako did a little twirl. The skirt swished up, betraying a glimpse of her skimpy undergarments. Whoops.

This was an attack with an instant-death effect for any son, but Masato gritted his teeth and survived. He nearly burst a blood vessel doing so.

"B-based purely on your face and figure, that's not half-bad, but speaking as your son, it's a big hell no! ...Plus, the skirt is way too short. Quit rolling up the waistband to raise the hem. Put it back where it should be, all the way down to your knees."

"Aww, but it's cuter short. You're such a harsh critic, Ma-kun."

"No need to demand cuteness from school uniforms. Don't bother."

He felt like a dad scolding his daughter about her skirt length. It was simply unacceptable to have a family member dressed this inappropriately.

Especially his mother... Masato was fighting off the urge for a joint suicide with all his might. Enduring stats like these were the only things he was successfully raising.

Calmly, he moved on to the next question.

"So. Explain why, exactly, you had to come to school dressed like this."

"Well, about that... You see, just as I'd tried on the uniform, I realized I had forgotten to include the chopsticks in your lunchboxes."

"Oh, really? That *is* pretty important."

"I know! So I figured I'd better get them to you right away and came all the way here without stopping to change... So here you go! Sorry Mommy is such a ditz."

Mamako handed him a box of chopsticks. "Well, thanks, then." You couldn't very well eat lunch without chopsticks. He was genuinely grateful.

No, wait. A thought crossed his mind.

"Say, Mom. I'm sure this isn't the case, but…you didn't deliberately leave the chopsticks out, thinking it would give you the perfect excuse to show up at school, did you? You wouldn't do that? Right?"

He kept a close eye on her reaction.

Mamako neither confirmed nor denied; she did an adorable little head tilt.

"I'm gonna need a yes or no response."

"Mm? Mm…mmm?" She was still trying to grin her way out of it.

He couldn't prove anything, but this was definitely intentional. He was sure she'd planned it.

But still, he forced himself not to yell at her. Masato was maturing. He had a big heart. Being able to eat his lunch was a good thing. All for the love of lunch. Lunch first.

Masato allowed himself a very large sigh and then accepted the situation.

"…All right, I'll allow it. Just this once."

"Thank you! I love it when you're nice to me, Ma-kun."

"Yeah, yeah… But honestly, if you've gotta show up, this is the way to do it. The damage done to me is still significant, and I mean *significant*…but if my own mother also showed up in the classroom I'd never live it down."

"'Also'? You mean…there are other moms in class?"

"Yeah. The lady we met yesterday, Medhimama. She barged in insisting she wanted to observe the class. Sat herself down between Medhi and me, getting in our way… I'm not too happy about it…"

"And what happened to Medhimama? Did security escort her away?"

"Nope. She was so pushy about it that she shoved Mr. Burly—who's way bigger than any security—right out of her way, and he was forced to allow it. Seriously the worst."

"Oh, I see… If you're just pushy enough…" Mamako thought about this. Seriously considering it. "If you're very, very pushy…" She started making arm movements like a sumo wrestler, even shouting "*Dosukoi!*" as if a match was about to begin.

Uh-oh. Masato had slipped up, and the result was clearly a precursor to danger. Parental emergency incoming.

"Um, Mom, I know you know better, but..."

"O-of course! I completely understand. If I did that, you'd hate me, right? I'd cry so much if you ended up hating me. I would never do that."

"Good, good, I'm glad you get it. Moving on. If we're done here, you'd better get back to the inn..."

"No, no," a new voice said, and not the lady from reception. "It would be a shame to send Mamako away. You simply must head for the front lines."

Peering through the window of the office was an eternally unperturbed nun. Sometimes she was a headmaster, sometimes a nun.

"What? Shiraaase...where'd you come from?"

"I don't appreciate you reacting as if you'd spotted a bug, but so be it. Seeing as a parent-related problem is occurring in the classroom you're in, I believe a burst of extreme meddling from your maximum-firepower party member is in order. Mamako, please act however you see fit. I will grant you the necessary permissions."

"Oh! Why, thank you!"

"W-wait just a minute... You can't! If you do that..."

The mood in class was about to get real weird.

"Right, let's get second period started! Would the person on duty give the order?"

"Certainly," Mamako said. "Very well, then... Everyone, rise! Bow! Take your seats."

The students all stood up, took a bow, and sat down.

"Continuing from first period..."

"Waaaaaaaaaaaaaaaaaaaaaaaaaaaaaaaaaaaaaaaaaaaaaait!" Masato yelled. Mr. Burly was trying to start class as if nothing was wrong, and Masato was not having it. He slapped his desk several times, doing his level best to stop this.

"Wh-what is it, Hero Masato? What's got you so upset?"

"I am way beyond 'upset'! Please, Mr. Burly! You must have noticed something amiss just now! The person giving the order wasn't even the one on duty! She's not even a student! C'mon!"

Masato waved both hands dramatically at Mamako, sitting next to him in her sailor uniform.

Mr. Burly gave Mamako a long, hard look.

"...She's clearly a student, isn't she?" he said.

"Is there something wrong with your eyes?! Yeah, okay, as her son, I've got to admit she does look like she belongs here, but let me be very clear! She is my mother! Understand?"

"Bwa-ha-ha! You certainly do seem to get a kick out of calling girls your age 'Mom,' young hero! ...Should I be taking you to the hospital?"

"You should not!! ...Argghh! Mom, please! You tell him!"

"R-right. It's important to be clear on these things. Mr. Burly, I do apologize, but I am actually Ma-kun's mother. My name is Mamako."

"Huh...?"

Mr. Burly gave Mamako another look over, which turned into a long stare... He still seemed like he didn't believe her.

"Um, so...you're *actually* Masato's mother?"

"That's correct. It's the honest truth... Oh, right, I do have my maternal and child health (MCH) handbook with me, if you'd care to look."

"Why're you carrying that around with you?! Who needs that once the kid's my age?!"

"Wow, you always carry those records around with you? You really are the hero's mother!"

"Yes. I just had to see how my son was doing at school, so I decided to join the class. I do apologize."

Mamako bowed low.

Mr. Burly took all this in, then nodded. "Mm, very well. Then I grant you permission to join the class." No reluctance at all.

"Hey!! Mr. Burly?!"

"Settle down, Masato. I can imagine how you must feel, but calm yourself and listen. I think—"

"You think what?"

"Spending time with your mother is, in fact, the main selling point of this game! The *MMMMMORPG* (working title). If a parent desires to be with their child, we should allow that to happen."

"No, but... The school rules said..."

"Rules were made to be broken!" Mr. Burly declared, raising a fist to the sky. "To protect my students' families, I'll take on the school, even the game admins! Even if they treat it as a bug, I'd gladly get patched out if it meant I'd fought for my students! I'm only a few kilobytes of data! There's no room in there for regrets!"

"That sure sounds cool, but it's also suuuuuper annoying... Wait, are those 'few kilobytes' compressed data? Even still, isn't that a little light for an entire life?"

Mr. Burly truly was the best teacher (past tense).

But then...

"If you're quite done," said a haughty, irate voice that grated on the ears.

It was Medhimama. She was at the back of the room, perched upon a specially prepared observer's seat as if she owned the place, and had clearly reached the limits of her patience.

"Mr. Burly, may I ask exactly what the meaning of this bizarre behavior is? Emphasis on 'bizarre.'"

"Huh? Bizarre how? I don't think..."

"Your behavior is entirely out of line! When I attempted to join the class, you did everything you could to prevent it, but with Mamako, your reaction was quite the opposite!"

"Well, that's because, on a basic human level, her qualities as a mother are much—"

"What did you say?!"

"N-nothing! I didn't... After the incident with you, I discussed things with the board, and the board representative gave the go-ahead for these things! Thus, we were able to prepare an observer's seat. Mamako is receiving no special treatment, so please calm yourself."

Mr. Burly was making himself as small as his physique allowed, bowing his head repeatedly.

Medhimama let out a long, exasperated sigh. Her anger remained, but she spoke in much calmer tones. "I hardly think that's likely, but I'll just leave that be for now. It would never do for me to delay the start of class any further than it already has been... Mamako, won't you join me? Parents and guardians sit over here."

"Yes, of course... Ma-kun, good luck! I'll be right behind you, watching your every move!"

"Just—don't! Hurry up and sit down!"

Mamako finally moved to the observers' seats. He really wished she wouldn't say things like that.

This was all the result of his failure to stop her invasion.

"*Pfft*, I totally called this," Wise said, giving him a very irritating smirk. Behind him, Porta was beaming happily. Masato was exhausted already.

I'm sure Medhi's laughing at me, too...

He glanced to his left. Yep. Medhi was doing just as Medhimama said, sitting one seat away, and she was quietly giggling into her hand. He was a laughingstock.

...I'm done... Just kill me now...

Right now, Masato would gladly accept any form of death. His emotions were in tatters.

And second period was just beginning.

"Despite no combat having taken place, we seem to have someone in critical condition, but I doubt anyone here can heal his wounds, so let's just get started. Continuing from first period, eyes up!"

Mr. Burly took chalk in hand and began writing on the board.

$6 - 7 (6 - 8)$

What was that?

"Just a quick review. The hero suggested that they face off in a round of tennis. Racket in hand, he faced the Demon Lord, managing to force a tiebreaker, but tragically lost. The defeated hero went to America to rebuild himself, but his sponsor said, 'That's not your job.' Remembering his duty, he took his sword in hand and returned to the Demon Lord's castle. That's where we left off."

"How did any of that make sense? Is there even an America here?!"

"Bwa-ha-ha! Since you slept through class, naturally you wouldn't understand! But that's what happened."

And the problem was...

"The hero used Divine Slash. But the Demon Lord took no damage."

...this again.

"I'm sure you're thinking, 'This again.' But it is! The main problem has yet to be resolved. If he does not find a way to drag the real Demon Lord out of his hiding space, he can never win. What now?"

When you got right down to it, this was a simple problem. There were plenty of potential answers, anything from the hero finding a way to the hiding space, to using a special item that undid the spatial distortion, but that range made it hard to answer.

Masato's party had to think about it. So did Medhi. A long silence filled the room.

This was not good.

I'm not liking this at all...

Was everyone but Medhi about to fall asleep, posed like they were thinking? That seemed likely. A lady at the back of the room could easily make that happen.

He glanced over his shoulder, and Medhimama had her staff in hand. She was already running interference.

But something wasn't right.

Hmm... Weird... Nothing's happening?

Medhimama was clearly trying to obstruct them, but the classroom hadn't changed. Masato, Wise, and Porta were all just fine, and none of the other students seemed to have fallen asleep, either.

Could this mean...?

Then Masato caught a gleam out of the corner of his eye.

Huh? Mom's elbow pad is glowing?

Medhimama waved the staff gently, and as she did, Mamako's elbow pad lit up.

Confused, Medhimama tapped her staff. Mamako's pad flashed. Nothing else happened. Medhimama waved the staff vigorously, twice. Mamako's pad flashed, twice. Nothing happened. Was this...?

Oh, is this...another mom thing?

It was.

This was that special mom skill where you made too much food and it would never do to let it go to waste so you shared the leftovers with the neighbors.

Mamako had absently activated the skill **A Mother's Sharing**, which allowed her to use her equipment's null status effect protection on others!

But even she hadn't noticed it. She was just happily waving back at him.

Next to her, the old bat was flailing her staff around wildly, snarling, "Wh-what in the...? Why isn't it working? C'mon!"

It was kinda hilarious.

"...*Pfft*... Toxic bitch... Serves you right..."

Did he hear something just now?

It seemed like it came from Masato's left, over where Medhi was sitting... No, no, there was no possible way. Words like those would never pass Medhi's lips. He must be imagining it.

Never mind.

At any rate, looks like Mom's saved us... Nicely done...

Masato wasn't upset about it. He found himself grinning, even. But he couldn't savor the victory just yet.

If he didn't need to worry about interference, then he could focus on the problem. Masato had to figure out an answer here.

But...

"Oh, I know!"

The first to raise their hand was none other than Mamako.

Masato's head throbbed. The whiplash from his good mood a moment before made his brain scream.

"Mom! Why are you trying to answer?"

"S-sorry. I just thought I might know…"

"Even if you do, you aren't allowed to answer! This is *our* class!"

"No, go ahead," Mr. Burly said. "Doesn't seem like any students have an answer, so let's hear what Mamako has to say. Special consideration, since she showed up in uniform!"

""Wha…?!"" yelped Masato and Medhimama as one.

Medhimama pulled up her window screen and quickly scrolled through her inventory…but it seemed like she didn't actually have a sailor uniform. Whew. Having even more mothers in sailor uniforms would be a living portrait of hell.

While she was preoccupied…

"Well, Mamako, what's your answer?"

"Oh, yes!"

The Demon Lord was hiding in another realm. What could be done? Mamako's answer…

"If he refuses to come out, you should go find the Demon Lord's mother and have her join you in asking him to come out. 'There's nothing to be afraid of. Mommy's right here. It'll be okay, so just come on out.'"

And hearing that, the Demon Lord would then say, 'Well, if Mom says so, it must be safe. Okay, I'm coming out,' and then come slithering out of whatever realm he'd hidden in…, she continued.

"Like hell he would!!"

"Hmm… Even the most evil criminals often respond to their mother's call. I doubt a Demon Lord would be any different! If his mother called for him, he'd have to come out. Good job, Mamako! Thirty points to you!"

"Oh my! I get points?"

"Whaaat?! That was right?! And why so many points?!"

"Then here's a problem for you, Mamako. The Demon Lord responds to his mother's call and emerges from hiding. The first thing he does is speak to the hero. What does he say?"

"Let's see… I suppose, 'Why are you with my mom? Get away from her!' That's definitely what Ma-kun would say if he was the Demon Lord."

"I would *not*! Why are you putting words in my mouth?!"

"Bwa-ha-ha! Clearly Hero Masato loves his mother! Correct! Thirty more points to Mamako!"

"How lovely!"

"How is that correct?!"

"Next problem! The Demon Lord Hero Masato plunges into battle to save Mamako, but..."

"Am I the Demon Lord or the hero here?! Actually, how 'bout you just leave me out of this entirely?! I'm not even involved here!! Ugh, anyway, let's just abandon the entire story line, okay?!"

But Masato's desperate cries fell on deaf ears.

Thanks to Mamako's unconscious support, Medhimama's ploys were completely foiled, and the rest of the class proceeded smoothly.

In a sense.

"...*Sigh*... Mom answered all the questions, got them all right, and made off with all the points...and got three times the points every time... Whyyy...?"

"Yeah... Was it moms get three times the points day or something...?"

"Nobody told us that?! And that's hardly a benefit to the kids, is it?"

More like unmitigated spite. But Mamako's point rate aside...

After school, it was time for students and guardians to go home together. Normally there wouldn't be any parents or guardians there, but since there were, they also had to go home. After all, what else were they going to do? Stay at school?

This was fundamentally different from a tough boss at the end of a high-difficulty quest, but the day had forced Masato to face harsh realities in a way that left him deeply worn-out.

But as they left, he spied the Cleric mother and daughter walking ahead of them.

Oh! I've had enough of Medhimama, but there's Medhi! The oasis of my heart!

She was the only one who could heal the exhaustion inside him.

Like a man dying of thirst in the desert, Masato ran up behind them, calling out to Medhi.

"Hey, Medhi!"

"Mm? Oh, Masato."

"On your way home?"

"Yes. We're headed back to our lodgings... Oh, right. Thank you again for today. With you there, I was able to really enjoy myself."

"O-oh, please! I didn't do a thing, really!"

Perhaps he should have said, "If you wish it, I'll always be by your side, milady," and he did seriously consider it but concluded that there was no way.

Then Medhimama suddenly forced herself between the two of them.

"Hey...!"

"That's quite enough small talk. Let us proceed."

"C-certainly, Mother... Masato, farewell."

"Ah... Aughhh..."

That was not nearly enough small talk. He was prepared to spend at least a few more minutes saying "See you again!" "Yes, tomorrow!" and earning himself the energy to live another day. He wanted to part with a smile.

But he couldn't even speak to her. Medhimama had her defenses raised and was guarding Medhi flawlessly, walking her quickly away.

Masato deflated.

"Argh... What the hell...? Am I cursed by all mothers or something...?"

That would explain it. Perhaps that was the only explanation that made sense.

Their first day of school had been entirely about mothers, in the worst possible way.

And the results of the day...

Masato: 0 SP. Wise: 0 SP. Porta: 0 SP.

Mamako, unofficially: 360 SP.

What are you doing, Mom?! Masato had already lodged numerous complains, but the results spoke for themselves.

Their week at school had only just begun. They had a long road ahead of them.

Report Card

Student: Masato Oosuki

Teacher: Mamako Oosuki

(I'm not the teacher, but this was the only place to write my name)

Academic Performance

Interested/Focused: Pays Attention, Actively Participates	✓
Speaking/Listening: Articulates Thoughts, Understands Those of Others	✓
Knowledge/Comprehension: Demonstrates These with Regards to Classroom Content	✓
Skills/Expression: Uses Imagination, Expresses Concepts with Their Own Sensibility	✓

Overall Academic Impressions

So engaged in class! I watched breathlessly from behind as he thought so hard!

I bitterly regretted not bringing a camera.

I will say I wish he was a little more polite when addressing Mr. Burly.

Notes from Parent or Guardian

I was asked to fill out this report card when I started observing the class, but will this do?

If there are any issues with it, let me know!

Gioco Accademia

Chapter 3 The Graffiti on That Wall Is a Beautiful Memory, but the Fist and Foot Marks Are Best Forgotten. We Should Really Get Rid of Those.

The second day of school.

Masato yelled, "Okay, we're off!" across the inn and started walking.

Faster and faster, like he was in a power walking race.

"Hey, Masato! Wait up! You're going too fast!"

"Masato, please wait! I want to walk with you!"

His party members' cries were enough to slow him down a little.

He turned to look back and saw Wise and Porta hustling after him. Just them. Safe for now.

Wise was whatever, but he did want to wait for Porta, so he waited till they caught up.

"Geez. You went off like a rocket! Ever heard of a li'l thing called *cooperation?*"

"Cooperation is nothing but a chain that ties me down. Even the greatest of the great understand that."

"Wait, what? That doesn't even make sense… Oh, hang on, Mamako still isn't here."

"I think we'd better wait for Mama…"

"Stop. Both of you. Please don't say another word."

Why had Masato left the inn in such a hurry? Why else?

There was no getting out of Mamako observing class. Her presence was also a big help to them, so that much he was forced to overlook. But going to school with her was out of the question. He would not stand for it.

Masato was supposed to be walking to school with someone else at his side.

This is no place for moms... I'm supposed to be here with my heroine!

Coincidentally bump into her on the way to school, chat about this and that, walk side by side... He knew just the angel to do that with.

Who? It's obvious, right? I need not say.

Masato pressed forward, hoping to be reunited with his destined partner, down the main road to the school.

And as he reached the corner of an intersection, he heard familiar voices coming from a side street.

"You overslept? Why, I never! Medhi! Hurry up! You have to be number one in everything! Including getting to school first!"

"Yes, Mother! I'll just go on ahead!"

Masato hurried into the intersection, glancing toward the voices. As he'd hoped, his heroine was running toward him.

Perfeeeeeect! Thank you, destiny!

This is it, this is it, this is it! It's reunion time! Masato prepared himself to enact the perfect coincidental encounter. He was totally prepared to act naturally. Here she came!

Medhi's head was down, not looking ahead of her at all.

"...Every time she opens her mouth it's just 'number one' this, 'number one' that... Shit... Gimme a break, you toxic bitch..."

Mm?

What was Medhi muttering? Was he hearing words like *shit* and *bitch*?

No. No, no, no, no. Masato's heroine would never be so foul-mouthed. This couldn't be. He must be hearing things. He was sure of it.

More importantly, there was the situation at hand.

...Oh! Is this what I think it is?

On the way to school. Beautiful girl running without looking ahead. With those conditions in mind, I hardly need explain the outcome. Yep. There was only one way this could play out.

And Medhi had premium-sized goods equipped up top.

Ba-dump, boing! If you know what I mean.

But that could only happen if they bumped into each other.

Masato had already realized they were on a collision course. It was technically possible for him to call out to Medhi and avoid the boing entirely. He could easily do that.

But...was that the right course of action?

"Of course it is. We'd avoid injury entirely. Right?" Masato asked, looking up at the sky. Addressing the heavens, the source of his beloved sword Firmamento's power. The heavens had chosen him as their hero, and they would surely respond to his call.

He was sure they would, but...

"Hmm, that's odd. No answer? What does that mean? Hmm."

He'd just have to wait for one. It wasn't that he was looking forward to the emotional boing he'd always dreamed of, but he was better off withholding judgment until the great powers above answered him. If they bumped into each other in the meantime, oh well.

Just then...

"...Mm?"

The ground beneath Masato's feet began to move. This was no earthquake. The shaking was extremely localized. "**A Mother's Fangs**?! Now?!" Indeed, it was.

Just before Masato and Medhi made contact, an earth spike shot upward at an incredible speed. This was a skill borne from a mother's love that could seek out her son's location wherever he was, no matter what situation he was in.

Since they were in the middle of town, the spike was a little smaller than usual, but having this appear right before his eyes was still unbearable.

"Augh! Look out!!"

Masato managed to avoid running straight into it, skidding to a halt, off balance. He almost fell over backward, but as he hastily bent his upper body to avoid collapse...

...*Boing!* He bumped into something. With his face. And that "something" was...

"Hee-hee. I caught you at last, Ma-kun! Gotcha!"

...his mother's large, pillowy, fragrant...you-know-whats.

"Nooo! Not these! The other ones!"

"What other ones? Um... I'm confused..."

"Oh, uh, no, never mind, forget I said anything."

He was supposed to have *boing*ed off Medhi, but he couldn't exactly tell his mom that... Oh, how convenient, a pillar of earth for him to punch. Thank goodness there was something to punch nearby.

About the time he put his two hundredth fist mark on the pillar, Medhi's face emerged from behind it. Beautiful. Pure. The image of perfection.

"...Oh, Masato. Everyone. Good morning."

"O-oh, Medhi. Mornin'. This thing sort of popped up out of nowhere. You aren't hurt or—"

"Medhi! Why have you stopped?! Get yourself to school right now!"

An irate voice cut Masato off. A flicker of annoyance crossed Medhi's face, but she did as she was ordered and ran off toward the school.

He considered calling after her, but he'd just get her yelled at again, so he let her go.

Wise and Porta caught up with Masato, and they waited for the boss character to arrive.

"Oh, hello, everyone. Do you know how to greet people properly?"

"Sure I do. Good morning."

"Mornin'."

"I know how to greet people, too! Good morning! Was that good enough?"

Masato's party stood face-to-face against Medhimama, who seemed to have caked on more makeup than she did yesterday. She didn't exactly come across as hostile, but there wasn't anything particularly welcoming about her, either.

Meanwhile, Mamako behaved just as she always did, greeting her with a smile. "Fancy running into you here, Medhimama! Will you be observing today, too?"

"I will. As will you, I see… But if I may make one thing perfectly clear, Mamako…"

"Yes? What is it?"

Medhimama fixed Mamako with a piercing glare. "I have prepared not only a sailor uniform but every other manner of garb I could conceive of! I will not allow you to monopolize things any longer! It will be Medhi and I who emerge victorious! There will be no repeat of yesterday!"

After this intense speech, she turned and walked away.

Mamako looked rather confused by this one-sided declaration of war and just stared blankly after Medhimama.

"U-um, Ma-kun? What was that about?"

"Just ignore her… Easier said than done, though… She's not really going to let us do that. We've drawn her aggro now."

Medhimama was hell-bent on supporting her daughter with a deeply obnoxious level of passion. And Masato's party would be the ones to pay the price. What could they do about it?

Masato called Wise and Porta over and held an emergency meeting.

"Umm, as you saw for yourselves just now, today's class is gonna be a mess again. We'd better go in with a plan."

"Wh-what? Don't we already have one?"

"Yes! With Mama there, Medhimama will be totally shut out! We can take the class in peace!"

"You have a good point, Porta… But remember, thanks to Mom's actions yesterday, she ended up taking all the points we were trying to earn. Hard to be happy about that, right?"

""Oh…""

Yep. After Mamako entered the classroom, she'd taken over and made off with all the points. That fact was inescapable. A light that shone too brightly could easily do more harm than good.

"So before anything else happens, we've got to turn the tables. Class today will be our show!"

"Okay! Let's do this!"

"Right! I'll do my best! I'll try so hard!"

Porta was super adorable when she got all worked up like this, but this was no time to savor that.

Masato flipped his own switch, getting fired up, and his party strode toward school, their auras clearly visible.

They were doing this. They had to do this.

With unbridled passion burning in their hearts, they took the day's class head-on!

"Okay, yesterday we mostly focused on combat, so today we're going to focus on crafting. It might be a little tough for you fighting types, but let's do our best."

""Waaaaaaaaaaaaaaaaaaaaaaaaaaaaaaaaaaaaaaaaaaait!""

Masato and Wise both grabbed their chairs, ready to throw them directly at Mr. Burly. "What? When did this become a school for delinquents?!" All schools have some, you know.

They calmed down a short while later.

They were gathered not in the classroom but in the food science lab. As the name implied, this room could handle both home economics and science lessons. The students were standing at tables covered in kitchen utensils and experiment apparatuses.

Observation seats were placed at the back of the class for Mamako and Medhimama.

Both were wearing sailor uniforms.

Ignoring those dangers…

Mr. Burly, though somewhat intimidated by Masato's and Wise's glares, pushed on with his explanation.

"Um, uhhh… A-anyway, we'll be crafting today. By actually experiencing Item Creation for yourselves, you'll learn about its effects."

"But, Mr. Burly, that's the problem."

"We're in combat jobs. We can't do Item Creation at all."

"I anticipated a certain degree of sulky complaints. But don't worry. This food science lab is designed to allow the Item Creation experience. The room is set to allow users of any job to perform crafting."

"Oh, really?"

"Geez, you shoulda said that first!"

"Bwa-ha-ha! I see you've cheered up! How easily...er, how responsive you all are. Anyhoo..."

His smile beaming forth again, Mr. Burly snapped his fingers.

A magic circle appeared around the podium, and a number of ingredients began appearing. Meat, fish, vegetables, fruit, grains, and spices.

"The objective will be to craft some food. This will make it easier for combatants to grasp the creation process. The apparatuses on each table are designed to raise your success rates, so make good use of them. Points will be given based on success rate and rarity. Those are what you're aiming for! Begin!"

And with that, the students set to work. Sorting through the ingredients on the podium, carrying them back to the tables, and setting about Item Creation.

Masato's party joined in.

"I've never done anything like this...but it doesn't seem like we've got anything to worry about."

"Yeah. We've got Porta on our side... So, wanna show us how it's done?"

"Okay! Leave it to me! I'll make something first!"

Porta put an egg in a random beaker and quietly chanted, "Will it be good? It'll be good! A good item...done!"

Light poured out of the beaker, and when it dimmed, there was a steaming egg inside.

Porta created Easily Peeled Boiled Egg—great success!

"Whoa... You sure made that look easy. Well done, Professor Porta."

"Th-thank you so very much!"

Like Porta had, Wise put an egg in a beaker and chanted.

"Will it be good? Well, duh, it'll be good! 'Cause I'm the one making it! So gimme a...boiled egg!"

Wise's Item Creation activated. Light poured out, and when it vanished...

…there was a greenish, purplish, reddish-brown slimy thing in the beaker.

Wise created Mysterious Object X!

"What the—? What even *is* this?! Eww, it stinks!!"

"Ohhh… Um, well… That's an Item Creation failure."

"Bwa-ha-ha-ha! That's your specialty, all right! Okay, my turn! …That cute little chant's not really my style, so I'll abbreviate a bit… Boiled egg, come on! …Uh, wait…"

The remains of a detonated egg appeared in the beaker in Masato's hand.

Masato created What Happens When You Try to Cook an Egg in the Microwave.

"Um… Well, that might be edible, at least. But, Masato, that's still a failure."

"Do you just lack any kind of common sense? That was total overkill."

"Hey! This is just what Item Creation did! Of course I know if you zap an egg in a microwave it'll explode! Argghh… Well, clearly, Item Creation won't succeed if you don't have a crafting job. Everyone else…"

He looked around, hoping to see them failing.

"Oh, nicely done, Cleric Medhi!" he heard Mr. Burly saying. "An excellent success rate! Ten points to you!"

Laid out on Medhi's table were fried eggs, scrambled eggs, an omelet, and several other successful egg dishes.

Medhi's job was Cleric, and she was registered as a combatant. Her success rate was frankly astonishing.

"Whoa, well done, Medhi! That's exactly why you're my heroine! Just how much more will you torment me?!"

"Hang on," Wise said. "Masato, look."

"Mm? You mean…?"

He followed Wise's glare to the back of the room. To Medhimama. Sailor uniform mom number two.

It had taken him a lot of nerve to look that way, and he regretted it immediately. He suffered through it.

Medhimama was stroking her staff. Clearly activating some sort of support effect.

"So I'm thinking," Wise said deliberately, "she may look all cool and perfect, but she's actually making a bunch of Mysterious Object X. And then that old bat is using an illusion spell to disguise them. That's what I think anyway."

"Whoa, whoa, hold up. That's quite an accusation."

"But not a baseless one. There's no magic that can raise Item Creation success rate. The other magic kids are all looking at her with great suspicion, so I bet I'm right."

Wise was right. There were a number of other students watching Medhi and frowning. The only one praising her was Mr. Burly. Everyone else was watching in frosty silence. A chill settled over the room.

But even then, even if that's what was going on, Masato would like to believe in Medhi's ability...

"Um, if I could... Rather than worry about other people, I think it's best if we try our hardest!" Porta said. "I think that's what's most important!"

Mm. She was right. The girl who always tried her best was totally correct.

"...Wise?" "Mmhmm, right." Wise pursed her lips but said nothing further about Medhi.

"We've gotta find a way to cook things successfully... How can we do that? I mean, Mom's really good at cooking, but I haven't heard anything about her making it with Item Creation... Wait, what? Where's Mom?"

Sailor uniform mom number one was not in the observation seats. Where had Mamako gone...?

"Ma-kun! Mommy's over here!" she called. He turned to look...

Mamako had donned an apron over her sailor uniform (where did she get that?) and had taken over a table, where she was hard at work.

She had some veggies on a board, and her knife was tap-tapping away. She slid the chopped veggies into a pot, applied a gem-fueled burner, and set it to boil.

Yep. She was just cooking.

"Uh, Mom? What are you doing?!"

"What else? I'm cooking! Watching you all made Mommy want to join in! I asked Mr. Burly, and he said it would be fine."

"I can't believe you're doing this again…!"

"Oh, right. Ma-kun, will you try some? I hope it tastes like home!"

Mamako poured a little of the broth into a tasting dish and held it out for Masato.

"S-stop that! It looks really hot! There's a lot of steam!"

"That's right, you always did have a sensitive tongue, Ma-kun. Then we'd better cool it down!" She blew on it.

"Wait!! You don't need to do that for me!!"

"Hmm, I think it's still too hot." She blew on it again.

"Please stop!! Everyone's looking!! …Argh, fine! I'll taste it! I'll just do it!"

He had no choice but to grab the cooled dish away from her and knock it back.

Masato's Item Creation success rate improved! Since Mamako blew on it twice, his success rate doubled!

"…Huh?"

"My, my! Looks like Mommy developed another special power!"

"No, no, no, no, this is way too arbitrary! It's just too much… On the other hand, this totally helps! Wise, Porta!"

"I would loooove to tease you about your Oedipus complex again, but right now we need to earn ourselves some points! Mamako, gimme some of the twice-blown broth!"

"Can you blow on mine, too?"

Wise and Porta each accepted a sample of Mom-Blown Broth and knocked it back. Both their success rates improved!

Now they had a shot.

"Let's do this! Bring all the stuff you want to use in a tasty dish!"

"Just throw it all into this success-boosting apparatus! Then!"

"I'll do the chant! …Will it be good? It'll be good! A good item… done!"

Item Creation activated. Blinding light poured out of everything they'd thrown into beakers, pots, and bowls. And…

The table was soon adorned with a thick, juicy steak; a wooden serving boat covered in seasonal sashimi; and a six-foot-tall wedding cake.

Mr. Burly took one look and his eyes nearly popped out of his head.

"Whoa! I didn't think you'd make anything like that! Consider me impressed! Hero Masato, Sage Wise, Traveling Merchant Porta! I'll give each of you twenty points!"

""""Yes!""""

So many points! So many emotions!

Masato's party was showered with praise. The students around them, Medhi included, applauded, smiling. Medhi seemed genuinely pleased for them. She was a great heroine indeed.

But Medhimama…

"…The nerve… Something must be done…"

…was glaring at Masato's party, and at Mamako, with naked hostility.

And, though perhaps not worth mentioning, she did this wearing a sailor uniform.

The crafting lesson had concluded, and it was lunchtime.

Masato's party was gathered in the sunny garden, sitting on a blanket and enjoying their meal.

"Didja see that old bat's face? She looked so pissed! It was *majorly* satisfying."

"You sure are spiteful… But yeah, I gotta admit I felt pretty good about it, too."

"Yes! Even I thought, 'Take that!'"

"You all tried so hard! And that got you good results. I'm so proud of you!"

"Yeah, we went for it. We really did. We worked really hard… maybe a little too hard."

Masato sighed, glancing down at their lunch.

On the menu was Mamako's handmade lunches, Mamako's handmade stew, thick juicy steak, a sashimi boat, and a six-foot-tall wedding cake for dessert.

So much food… So many calories… "…Can we get through it all?" "I think we have to." "I'll do my best!" "Don't force yourself." Chopsticks moved quickly, making headway.

A hero, a hero's mother, a Sage, and a Traveling Merchant. A party working together, battling to consume sliced steak and sashimi with the rice from the lunches.

Hmm… We're in a game! What are we even doing?

Masato shook his head.

Just then…

"My, that's quite a spectacular lunch."

At this familiar voice, they looked up to find a woman dressed as a nun. Shiraaase.

"Oh, Ms. Shiraaase! Won't you join us?"

"Would you mind? I certainly wouldn't mind partaking in a few… Oh, but first I suppose I should take care of business. Mamako, if you could join me for a minute?"

"Yes? What is it?"

Shiraaase beckoned, so Mamako got up and went over to her.

Shiraaase quietly spread her arms and gave Mamako a big hug.

Masato did a spit take. Everything in his mouth went flying.

"*Pffft… Cough, cough…* Wha…? Shiraaase?!"

"I, too, am happily married and have a child, Masato. What you see before you is your mother being embraced by another mother. How does that make you feel?"

"My brain is refusing to function, so I can't say!"

"Fair enough. Even I am uncertain as to what the selling point of this situation actually is. I believe that's enough. Mamako, thank you."

"Um, okay? I don't really get it, but as long as I was helpful…?"

Shiraaase released Mamako, and the two of them sat down on the blanket.

As if nothing out of the ordinary had happened, Shiraaase began eating. Starting with the wedding cake. Just cutting herself a generous slice.

She sure packed it away, but that was pretty much expected behavior from her at this point. They all waited.

"...How about an explanation? What exactly was that demonstration for?"

"Nothing significant. I just had a need for a rough size estimate and chose that method of conducting it."

"You needed her size?"

"Yes... I am somewhat reluctant to discuss this matter in front of Wise, but..."

"Oh, I see where this is going! Fine! One more word outta you and this steak platter goes right in your face!"

"Whoaaa, it's hot! Don't do that!"

Incidentally, the steak platter was also completely flat. No lumps at all.

"At any rate, given the size requirements, I needed to ascertain whether Mamako would be able to wear something or not."

"Um. Wear...what, exactly? Y-you're not going to put her in another weird outfit, are you?"

Alarms were going off in Masato's head. His pulse jumped to unhealthy levels. Something horrible was about to go down...at least, something that would cause a great deal of suffering for him as her son. A wave of anxiety threatened to end him.

Shiraaase smiled faintly, as if enjoying his reaction.

"I recommend eating well to prepare for this afternoon's class. If you don't have a substantial reserve of energy, you may not be able to make it through! ...Heh-heh-heh..."

"What does that have to do with this afternoon's class?! By 'may not be able to make it through,' you just mean it'll be a difficult lesson, right?! That's what you're talking about, right?! Please just tell me that's what you're talking about!!"

"Oh my, lunch time is just about over. I must get back to debugging the school. So long! …Heh-heh-heh…"

"Um, Shiraaase? Shiraaaseeeeee?!"

Without even a passing glance, Shiraaase walked off with the cake.

Something was definitely going down.

The bell rang, and the afternoon class began.

They were gathered in the indoor pool. A large pool, with several fifty-meter lanes, and the students had all changed into the suits the school required—school swimsuits.

Masato alone was curled up in the stands by the side of the pool.

Abject depression. It was all too easy to tell what was about to happen.

Swimsuits… And definitely ones no normal mother would ever wear…

Mamako would definitely show up here. To swimming lessons. In a swimsuit. That's why Shiraaase had taken her measurements.

Mom. In class. In a swimsuit. It was a death sentence.

"No other hero in history has been this tormented by fate. Even if I fail to overcome it, no one in the world would blame me. The Demon Lord himself would pity me."

It must have been so tough! That's enough. You can rest now. He could almost see the Demon Lord patting his shoulder. He really thought he deserved that.

Reality was harsh. Nothing had even happened yet, but Masato was already teetering on the brink. His party members were calling him.

"Hey, Masato! What are you doing? Hurry up and get in line!"

"Masato! You aren't feeling sick or anything, right? Hang in there! Let's get some points!"

Wise and Porta were both in school swimsuits.

Wise was…well, she was curvier than that steak platter anyway. Porta, of course, was adorable beyond measure, and the way she was keeping her bag balanced on her head was just too cute.

But even with Porta encouraging him—Wise didn't really factor in—Masato didn't have the energy to stand.

But then...

"Um... Masato, are you okay?"

"Huh? ...Oh..."

Medhi had spoken to him. In her school swimsuit, she looked every bit as beautiful and pure and angelic as ever.

She was leaning slightly forward, peering into his face, and her rather large treasures were jiggling right before Masato's eyes.

Mm. What else could he ask for in life?

There were times when a man just had to rise to the occasion. No, not that way. Phrasing. Point is, he got to his feet. To claim those treasures.

"Um, Masato...?"

"Oh, um, don't worry, I'm fine! Totally fine! Sorry for making you worry!"

"Oh, good. Let's try to enjoy this class!"

Medhi smiled and walked away. Jiggling. "...Wise could never manage that."

"What are you looking at?" She stomped on his foot really hard and it hurt. A lot.

Even so, he couldn't very well look pathetic in front of his heroine, so Masato was back in action. He steeled his ragged nerves and lined up with the other students.

A moment later, Mr. Burly came dragging a whiteboard over to them.

"Right, everyone's here! And you're all suited up! Good, everything's in order! Naturally, I'm in my swimsuit, too! As you can see!"

Mr. Burly gestured proudly at his loincloth, as if to insist a loincloth was all the swimsuit a man could ever need.

But nobody enjoyed the sight, so they all ignored it.

"Bwa-ha-ha! Lots of you are averting your eyes, but you can't be a teacher if you're sensitive to these things! That said, I have been known to remember them later and weep quietly into my pillow."

For all his steely muscles, it seemed his mind was made of tofu. "I'd better explain what this class will be. Eyes on the whiteboard!"

The theme of the class was Waterside Training.

For combatants, monsters would appear in the pool, and they would fight them. They'd be ranked based on the number of enemies defeated, and the rarity of them, and the top-ranked student would get points.

For those with crafting jobs, they would be creating items from the materials the monsters dropped. They would be ranked based on the success rate and rarity of items created.

The combatants would defeat monsters and gather the drops. The crafters would take those drops, make items, and distribute them to the combatants. The combatants would use those items to fight more effectively. The key to this whole exercise would be both parties working in harmony to achieve the greatest results.

"And one more important factor! Don't worry if the monsters that appear belong in fresh or salt water! Just accept them as is! Got it?"

""""Right!""""" everyone said, agreeing to the unwritten rule.

With the explanation complete, Mr. Burly suddenly began to look nervous.

"Um, so as class begins, there's someone I'd like to introduce you to. Come on, boys! Ready? Let me introduce you to..."

"Me, of course!" Medhimama said forcefully.

Her lustrous, slim, youthful body was clad in a gold bikini.

Medhimama strode confidently past the students, her chest puffed out as if daring them to ogle it. "You look amazing, Mother!" Medhi cheered, clapping her hands.

But...

"Yes. Thank you. If we can get back to the point..."

"Wha...? Mr. Burly! Just as the male students are all in a frenzy...?!"

"""""...Sigh...""""" Everyone slumped.

"H-hey! You there! Why did you just sigh? Why are you all hanging your heads?! Look at me! At my swimsuit! Does it not thrill you?! Come, cheer for me!"

"All right, let's get Medhimama out of the way... And now, ladies and gentlemen!"

The one he'd meant to introduce was, of course...

"Hi, everyone! I'm Ma-kun's mother, Mamako! I hope you all work very hard!"

Mamako.

A mom. In a school swimsuit.

An actual mom. In a real school swimsuit.

For a moment, nobody there knew how to process this spectacle.

But she was large where it counted, and she was Mamako, after all.

"""""Woo-hoo! Welcome, school-swimsuit Mamako!"""""

The male students erupted with cries of joy. Each time the bounty mounted on her chest swayed, something stirred within them!

At the edge of this commotion, Masato was attempting to expel all the air from his lungs, dive to the bottom of the pool, and cling to it for the rest of his life.

If it was just a regular swimsuit... If it was anything but a school swimsuit...

After seeing something like this, as her son, as a human being, as an organic life-form, he simply could not go on living.

As Masato attempted to convert himself into an unknown mineral at the bottom of the pool... "Masato!" "What are you doing?!" Porta and Wise dragged him back up. It was a very sad sight.

"Um, quiet down, class," Mr. Burly said, wincing. "Calm down. Particularly you, hero. Take a deep breath and learn to live on dry land."

"Gah... Shiraaase... How could you...? You're a menace..."

To a son, there could be nothing worse than the sight of his mother in a school swimsuit. Like a virulent poison that affected only the eyesight and brain. The corruption may not prove fatal, but he would suffer all the same.

For Masato, even though it had its own problems, Medhimama's swimsuit was much...

No, maybe not. A mom waltzing into a place like this in a gold bikini and self-destructing wasn't exactly...

"...Heh-heh... Toxic bitch... Serves you right... That was funny as hell..."

"Gotta say I feel the same way... Wait..."

He replied without thinking, but who said that?

He glanced toward the voice and found his angel, Medhi.

"What's wrong, Masato?"

"Huh? Uh, no, nothing..."

Had Medhi said that? No, there was no way.

She was a beautiful girl. She'd never be so foulmouthed, or say anything like "That was funny as hell." She wasn't Wise!

"Geez... Wise, you shouldn't go calling people 'toxic bitch.' Even if it's true, it's rude to Medhi!"

"Huh? What?"

Wise look baffled, but she was clearly just playing innocent. Whatever. It didn't matter.

Medhimama was getting even more heated, yelling, "What's the meaning of this? It doesn't make sense! I'm being treated horribly compared to Mamako! Mr. Burly, explain yourself!"

"Now, now, you're just imagining it! It's all in your head! The observation seats are right over there! If the class can't proceed smoothly, I'm sure that'll affect your daughter's results, so if you wouldn't mind..."

"Argh! ...Y-you have a point! I'll quiet down for now, I suppose! Reluctantly!"

Scowling like a demon, Medhimama stalked over to the stands and sat down.

"Mamako, over here! Next to me!"

"R-right! If you'll excuse me."

"Hmph! ...I can certainly see that you're a beautiful woman and have taken very good care of yourself, but so have I! And yet...so frustrating!"

Medhimama's grumbles showed no signs of subsiding, but there was no point in paying them any attention.

Class was starting.

*   *   *

Masato and the other students scattered around the poolside. The combatants had weapons in hand, and the crafters were ready for Item Creation, everyone waiting for the signal.

"Ready...set...go! When I say that, you can start. Just kidding! Bwa-ha-ha!"

All students registered Mr. Burly as an enemy and targeted him right then and there. Mr. Burly had drawn all aggro in the room. His defeat was assured. "Whoa, sorry?! I'm a bit of a prankster!" Being a prankster would not earn him forgiveness.

"W-well then, for real! Ready...go!"

At last they got started. The combat students all jumped into the pool.

A lot of monsters spawned in the water. Monster fish, invertebrates like octopuses and squids, and even some sort of living seaweed. All sorts of aquatic creatures.

Yep. Exclusively aquatic monsters.

"Mr. Burly! I don't suppose there will be any flying monsters?"

"Oh, no. I mean, this class is for monsters found near water. So only aquatic."

"I figured as much, but arghhhhhhhh!"

Masato was specialized in fighting aerial foes and was not going to impress anyone here. But it was too soon to give up entirely. Masato wrangled his emotions into some semblance of enthusiasm and joined the fight.

But he didn't jump right into the water. He couldn't do that here. The poolside was packed with other students.

He needed to get himself in the middle.

If I leap off the diving board and swim a few strokes, I'll secure a good hunting spot!

He ran along the side of the pool (No running in the pool area!) and headed for the diving board.

His route took him past the observation seats.

"Oh, there's Ma-kun! Ma-kun! Mommy's right here! Good luck!"

Medhimama scowled at him, but Mamako smiled, waving.

Cheered on by his mom in a school swimsuit. He puked blood.

"...Guh..."

"Eeek! M-M-Ma-kun?!"

Masato began to collapse...

But out of the corner of his eye, he saw Wise go off the diving board into the pool.

"Ha-ha! You lie there and die, I'm going on ahead!"

"Ah! Wait! I had my eye on it first! Damn!"

The damage from school-swimsuit mom was dire, but this was no time for dying!

And his other rival...

"Masato! Pardon me!"

...was Medhi. She was also aiming for the center of the pool.

Medhi's dive was flawless, a sleek arc transitioning smoothly into a perfect crawl. The water pressure built up by her endowments proved no obstacle, and she made great time. "Wha...?! She's fast!" Wise said, quickly passed despite having negligible water pressure to contend with herself.

And when Medhi reached a fish monster, she took the staff in her hand...

...and clubbed it!

"Hahhh!"

Thunk! One shot. The head caved in, and the monster died instantly. It floated sideways and turned to dust.

"Wha...? You're finishing it with physical attacks, not magic? Medhi, are you a melee healer?"

"Yes! I'm a healer specialized in bash damage! Mother said I should be the ultimate being, a healer who challenges the assumption that healers aren't strong!"

"She's an educational master... I can't help being impressed...but I can't stand here gawking!"

Masato jumped into the pool himself. He pushed through the water, and as a monster approached—"First one!"—he slashed an octopus in two.

Masato defeated the octopus. Received item: Octopus Arm.
It was literally an octopus arm.

"Oh, materials! Hey, Porta! Where are you? Take this!"

"Here! I'm right here! Leave it to me!"

Masato tossed the material to her. Porta caught it beautifully. Time for Item Creation.

Porta took the Octopus Arm in hand and did her cute little chant. The visuals were alarming, but the chant made it cute.

"Will it be good? It'll be good! A good item...done!"

Light poured out of Porta's hands, and when she opened them...

Takoyaki flour, eggs, water, salad oil, and diced octopus arm. She also had a hot plate with lots of round depressions.

Porta created Takoyaki Party Set!

She'd gone to all the trouble of making it, but Masato was less than impressed.

"Wh-what is that...?"

"A Takoyaki Party Set! It lets me make takoyaki, which can recover status ailments! I'll make some right away!"

"S-sure... Just...don't burn yourself..."

"That sounds like fun!" Mamako said. "Mind if I join you? If we mix store-bought *chuno* sauce (a sauce made from a blend of fruits and veggies) and *mentsuyu* (a soup base typically used in soba and udon dishes), we can get a sauce every bit as good as the specialty sauces. The dashi in the *mentsuyu* really makes the flavors pop!"

"Yikes, look who took the bait..."

"All right, let's get cooking!" Wise said, joining them. "I'm great at flipping them!"

Takoyaki Girls Club @ Poolside had officially launched. School swimsuit takoyaki cooking by the pool. What was even going on...?

And wasn't Wise supposed to be defeating enemies? Masato was puzzled, but then he realized...

Oh... Did she get her magic sealed already...?

He hadn't noticed, but it was entirely possible... He could totally see her choking back tears, desperately distracting herself by mixing takoyaki ingredients. Poor thing.

But whatever, it was just Wise.

"This is a competition, so don't call me heartless for it! You can't blame me here!"

One less rival was something to be welcomed.

All he had to worry about was his one remaining rival, Medhi.

"Hey, Medhi! You're sure working hard!"

"Yes! Losing is simply not an option. Even if I'm up against you, I won't go easy!"

"I like that passion! Let's see who wins!"

He regretted not getting fired up enough to add an "I love you," but he had bigger fish to fry.

The number of monsters in the pool was steadily dropping. Medhi had been cleaning up. She had a pretty solid lead on him by now.

It would be tough catching up, but he wasn't ready to admit defeat just yet.

"There must be one somewhere! Now's my chance to turn the tables! A special bonus enemy or... Mm...?"

Something caught the corner of Masato's eye.

A large shadow in the pool. Much, much bigger than any of the other monsters, swimming along, its body writhing.

That was definitely a special enemy. It better be anyway.

"Right! That's what I've been waiting for! This is my chance! ...Medhi! Sorry, but I'm taking that one down!"

"No, I won't let you! I'll defeat it!"

Masato swam after the shadow. Medhi started swimming, too. The two were evenly matched, in a dead heat.

Just then...

"Ma-kun! Don't push yourself too hard! The scores don't really matter! What matters most is that you don't hurt yourself!"

"Medhi! You know what to do! You must be number one, no matter what! If you aren't number one, there's no point! You can't let that Masato kid beat you!"

Both moms' voices echoed across the water. One asking only for her child's safety. One asking only for her child's victory. Both cries revealing everything about the speakers.

Meanwhile, their children...

"Argh! You say that, and now I've gotta work twice as hard! Geez!"

Masato swam even faster.

Of course he did. If he slacked off after being told not to push himself, it would be like he was letting Mamako spoil him. Please. He didn't have an Oedipus complex!

But deep down...

...*My mom really does care about me.*

A part of him was pleased by this reminder. It wasn't a bad feeling at all, not that he wanted to admit it. Best to forget it.

Meanwhile, Medhi slowed down. She was gradually falling behind. Why...?

Then he heard Medhi whisper, "Ughhh... 'Number one, number one'... You're so obnoxious... Just drop dead already..."

"...Huh?"

Masato definitely heard that whisper. No doubt about it.

Medhi, his shining beauty...had a storm cloud cast over her expression. Her eyes went dark, like she'd lost faith in everything. She looked beyond irritated, her teeth grinding.

W-wait... What is this...?

Had he misheard her? Was he seeing things? No, this was rock-solid reality.

The oasis of Masato's heart, the angel he'd found at last, the heroine he was destined to meet had turned into something else entirely.

And then the shadow suddenly surfaced.

"Nyrrrrrrrrrrrrrr!"

He wasn't sure if that was a voice or just a sound.

The monster was a sea anemone as large as a tree. It towered over them, dozens of tentacles sprouting out of its upper torso, all of them wriggling and writhing. It was really creepy, and it smelled even worse.

The giant anemone got the first attack.

"What?! Already?!"

"Wha...? Eeek?!"

A number of thin tentacles stretched out, bearing down on Masato and Medhi as they stared in horror...!

Or so they thought. "...Huh?" The swarm of tentacles suddenly changed direction. "Mm?" They passed over Masato's head. "Hey, that's..." Stretching and stretching.

The tentacles attacked Mamako at the Takoyaki Party, where she'd been cheering Masato on.

"Oh? Oh, oh, oh?! Eeeek?!"

"Hey! Why're you targeting my mom?!"

The reason was unclear...but it was likely just because she was a mom.

In all of human history, there were extremely few instances of tentacle attacks on moms. Perhaps that's why the giant anemone decided to go for her.

To leave its mark on history.

"Nyrrrrrrr! Nyuuurruu!"

The tentacles completely ignored the panic-stricken merchant girl and the takoyaki-gobbling high school Sage, wrapping exclusively around Mamako's body!

Slimy tentacles around her arms, feet, and thighs!

The boldest of the tentacle tips were slipping under the edges of the swimsuit, the bastards!

Ah! Th-they were coming out! The swimsuit was being pulled aside and the parts that should be hidden were on full display!

"Nooo! There's something slimy and wriggly all over meee! It feels so weeeird! ...Ma-kun! Mommy's being attacked by lots of slimy things! Eeek!"

"Arghhh!! That's enooooooough!!"

This was unacceptable. Completely unacceptable. The situation, Mamako's voice, everything. Masato turned to rescue her when...

"Hold it!" Medhimama's voice rang out.

She was glaring furiously at the giant anemone.

"You there, what is the meaning of this? Why are you only targeting Mamako? ...She's not the only beautiful mother here! Wouldn't you say I am far preferable to Mamako? You would, right?"

Medhimama puffed up her chest, encouraging the tentacles to come after her.

It was unclear where the anemone's face was, but it clearly took a long look at her, then turned away. "What?!" Obviously not interested. Mamako won this popularity contest... Her son had no idea how to handle any of this.

He...he couldn't think about that now.

"Mama! Here!"

"Thanks, Porta! ...Mommy's gonna punish this bad, slimy tentacle monster!"

Mamako took Altura from Porta and held it high. The Holy Sword of Mother Ocean responded to her motherly rage, unleashing its overwhelming power.

Instantly, all the water in the pool concentrated into a massive spiral, launching the giant anemone upward. The monster's massive form flew through the air—the perfect place for Masato to attack.

"Good, good, good, good! Leave flying enemies to meeeeee!"

Masato swung Firmamento with all his might.

The beam locked onto the target, and the sleazy foe was sliced completely in two.

The practical exam in the pool concluded, Mr. Burly was announcing results.

"Allow me to list the top scorers! In third, the Knight, Male Student Number 3! Five points! Then in second, the Cleric, Medhi! Ten points! And right at number one...the hero, Masato! Thirty points! Congrats! A round of applause!"

""""Whoaaaaa! Masato, niiiiiiiiiice!""""

"Uh, thanks."

As everyone cheered, Masato did a slow circle, bowing repeatedly.

The number of foes Masato had defeated was nowhere near Medhi or the other students, but the rarity of the foe he'd felled had scored him a huge bonus, and nobody was arguing with his placement.

He was number one with a bullet. And he'd finally scored some decent points. It would have taken a lot of hard work and level-ups to store this many points, but now they were his!

But as excited as everyone else was, Masato himself was unenthused. He could hardly get worked up about this.

His mind was on other things.

...That stuff I heard earlier was some kind of mistake, right?

What preyed on Masato's mind was, of course, Medhi. He'd seen her face for only a moment...but the angry hiss she'd let out, the gloomy look on her face...he couldn't get it out of his mind.

He glanced her way, and she looked just like she always did. His ideal heroine, smiling like an angel, looking at him with admiration...

"Masato, congratulations! The way you beat that rare monster with one hit was really cool! I couldn't take my eyes off it!"

"Huh?! I—I was cool? Y-you couldn't take your eyes off...? Wow... Um... Thanks."

Praise like that certainly brought a warmth rising from deep within, but the other thing was still bugging him, so that warmth soon died down. He failed to get entirely carried away.

What now?

What was going on there? I should probably just ask her, but...

How could he broach the subject? He couldn't exactly just ask straight up, "Hey, did you, like, totally snap a minute ago? What was that about?"

As Masato frowned, losing himself in thought...

"Ma-kun! Congrats!"

"Eeep?!"

This again? The woman who refused to understand her son's feelings came running in and put her arms around his head, pressing it firmly into her chest. In her swimsuit. Unbearably soft.

"Mmf! Mom! Stop that! Everyone's looking!"

"Oh, just give me a minute! I'm so proud of you! You got a lot of points! Isn't that nice? Mommy's so happy for you!"

"Hang on, I thought you didn't know anything about SP? Let's not make a big fuss about things you don't even understand."

"Oh, that'll never happen. I am a mom, after all!"

"I have no idea what that's supposed to mean."

There was a lot she was unclear on, but it was clear enough her son was being rewarded, and that was cause for celebration. That's just how moms work, you know?

Porta came over, looking up at Masato with respect. *Gasp.* Perhaps the greatest reward of all.

"Masato! Congratulations!"

"Oh, thanks. Same for you, Porta! You were top crafter, and you got thirty points, too!"

"Yes! I am delighted!"

Porta threw both hands up in celebration, which was just too adorable for words.

"Up you go!" "Eep!" Masato grabbed her and hoisted her onto his shoulder.

With that done, what's next? Maybe he shouldn't poke a sore spot, but...

Wise was standing around, pretending she didn't care.

"Hmph! Well, I ate three plates of takoyaki! There are eight pieces a plate, so that's twenty-four whole pieces! Beat that!"

"Hmm... Well, if saying that doesn't make you depressed, who am I to judge?"

"*Gulp...* I'm not crying... I refuse to cry..." Tears streamed down her face.

Maybe best to pretend not to notice how desperate she was to maintain her dignity. Just don't look at her.

He didn't have time for Wise right now. He had to focus on Medhi.

Masato turned around, looking for her...

"I told you over and over, you have to be number one! And now look what happened! You should be ashamed of yourself!"

*   *   *

A hysterical scream followed immediately by a loud crack.

That mother had just slapped her daughter's cheek. And the daughter was just standing there and taking it.

"How dare you tell him he was cool!! You lost!! And then you go complimenting the one who beat you? Have you lost your mind?!"

"I—I just thought he was really strong and impressive…"

"Don't you dare talk back to me! Repent in silence!"

"Y-yes, Mother… I'm sorry…"

"Honestly… I've never been so disappointed… *Sigh…* That's enough. Enough. Go train yourself somewhere until after school. I'm doing this all for you, you know. Got that?"

"…Yes… Just as you say, Mother…"

With that final order, Medhimama stalked away, clearly still fuming.

Left behind, Medhi stared at her feet for a while and then turned and ran off, flying out the emergency exit.

Masato's party was left staring after her.

"Wait, I shouldn't just be standing here. I'm gonna go check if she's all right!"

"Oh, wait, Ma-kun! Mommy's coming, too!"

"Argh, you don't need to come, Mom! Geez!"

He considered stopping to deal with her, but time was of the essence. Let her do what she wanted. Masato ran after Medhi.

Where had Medhi gone? He couldn't find her. She had too much of a lead on him.

When Masato and Mamako reached the exit, they split up. "I'll go right!" "Mommy will take the left!"

Masato went clockwise around the outside wall of the indoor pool but found no signs of Medhi.

"*Tch!* Not this way, hunh? Then Mom picked right?"

He went back the way he'd come, counterclockwise along the wall.

And ahead of him he saw a school swimsuit–clad butt… No, don't look at it. That's your mom's.

Mamako was bent over at the corner of the building, peering around the corner.

"Hey, Mom. What're you doing?"

"Oh, Ma-kun! Good timing. Take a look here…"

Mamako made room for him. He couldn't get a read on her expression.

That bothered him, but he figured it was best to take a look for himself.

…*Mm?*

That was Medhi all right. Definitely here. It was her, but…

"…Argh… Pisses me off… Take that! And that!"

Medhi was kicking the wall of the building over and over. *Thump. Thump.* Like she was stomping it. Your classic yakuza kick.

Was he seeing this? Did his eyes deceive him? Was he hallucinating? All these possibilities seemed likely, but perhaps that was just wishful thinking.

He looked again, and Medhi was still yakuza kicking the hell out of the wall. Looking extremely unhappy. *Thud, thud, thud, thud, thud, thud, thud, thud, thud.*

"Arrghh… I seriously wanna kill that toxic bitch…"

He'd heard her talk like that before. All those half-heard hisses. Guess they were Medhi after all.

Some things in the world you're better off not knowing. Mysteries of the world, secrets that endanger your very life.

The dark side of a beautiful girl was one of these.

This can't be true… Someone, please tell me it's not true…

He'd believed she was an angel. Not a fallen one.

He longed to gouge his eyes out and pretend he'd never seen this.

But he also couldn't just leave her to it…and Mamako was giving him a shove, as if to say, "Ma-kun, give it a shot!" Like, now, of all times, she wanted him to take the lead. Oh well.

"Um… *Ahem.* Gosh, where could Medhi be?" he said, sounding *totally* natural. "Is she over here?"

He gave her a minute to compose herself and then stepped around the corner.

And found...

"...Oh, Masato. Mamako, too!"

Medhi turned to face them, looking like the absolute picture of beauty and purity, as if nothing out of sorts had just happened.

"What brings you both here? Were you looking for me?"

"Huh? Um, yeah, more or less."

"We were worried, so we thought we'd come check on you."

"Oh... Sorry to cause you any concern. I'll be fine. As you can see."

Medhi smiled brightly. If it weren't for the slight swelling on her check, she'd seem exactly like she always did.

Like always...but she definitely had a dark side...but he couldn't exactly ask, "Are you broken inside?"

So he elected to act normal.

"Um, can we talk? I couldn't help noticing... Is your mother always like that?"

"Yes, that's pretty typical."

"So she's always all 'Be number one,' and if you aren't number one...she gets all mad and slaps you?"

"Yes. That's my mother for you."

Medhi nodded as if that was normal. As if she had no concerns about her mother's behavior at all.

When Masato and Mamako were at a loss for words, Medhi took the lead.

"Do you two think my mother's an awful person?"

"Um, well. If I'm being totally honest, I think 'awful' is an understatement. I'd go more with 'reprehensible.'"

"Ma-kun! That's going too far!"

"I'm only telling the truth. You can't just smack people like that."

"Well... I'm not saying I'm in favor of corporal punishment... but..."

"I don't mind. Everyone who sees her acting like that says the same thing as you, Masato. They all say she's horrible. But..."

Medhi paused, searching for words. Then she smiled again.

"But that's fine. I don't care what they say. It's fine."

"Uh, doesn't seem like it. I mean, how is this fine?"

"Yes," Mamako said. "I'm afraid I don't think it seems exactly fine, either."

"But it is," Medhi said. "Mother doesn't do this because she hates me. She's strict with me because she's thinking about what's best for me, and she's trying to raise me right. I know that much is true. I trust my mother."

Her expression was grave as her words were clear. This didn't seem like a lie.

"So don't worry about me. I'll be fine... I'm sure my mother will cause a commotion again, but we'll only be together for a few days, so please...just put up with it. I know it's a lot to ask."

With this request, she politely bowed her head and turned to leave.

Masato and Mamako couldn't bring themselves to stop her. They just stood and watched her go.

"...What do you think, Mom?"

"Well... It seems like Medhi really cares about Medhimama... If this were a mom interview, I'd want to give her a gold star..."

"If that were all there was to it, sure. But..."

"Yes, indeed..."

The two of them looked at the wall, covered in scuffs from the brutal kicking it had endured.

It was beyond doubt that Medhi both cared deeply about her mother and had some much nastier feelings lurking below the surface.

"...What do we do?"

"...What *do* we do?"

Both mother and son sighed as one.

The curriculum for the day over, the results were published.

Masato: 50 SP. Wise: 20 SP. Porta: 50 SP.

If you counted each takoyaki she'd eaten as one point, Wise drew within shooting distance of the other two, but considering that also made her number one in calories consumed for the day, and the moment she realized that she quickly started doing sit-ups... Well, that's a story for another day.

Their scores were certainly appreciated, but the second day of school had left them with other things on their minds.

Report Card

| **Student:** Wise |
| **Teacher:** Mamako Oosuki (Filling in) |

Academic Performance

Interested/Focused: Pays Attention, Actively Participates	✓
Speaking/Listening: Articulates Thoughts, Understands Those of Others	✓
Knowledge/Comprehension: Demonstrates These with Regards to Classroom Content	✓
Skills/Expression: Uses Imagination, Expresses Concepts with Their Own Sensibility	✓

Overall Academic Impressions

It was so memorable how she threw herself into eating takoyaki after her magic got sealed! She might need to take care not to overeat.

I think it's good for children to have healthy appetites.

You so often see girls eating like birds!

I was very impressed by how heartily Wise ate.

Notes from Parent or Guardian

I'm writing this in place of Wise's actual mother, Kazuno.

Gioco Accademia

Chapter 4 Mom's Baggage Had a Food Sanitation Notebook. No Signs of a Chef's License.

The third day.

Mamako included, everyone went to school together.

"Ugh… Like she belongs here…and she's even sitting next to me…"

"Just until class starts! And Mr. Burly gave his permission to observe the class… But, well… If you really don't want me here, I could go back to the inn."

"And so, rejected by her son, Mamako sat alone in their room, her head down, looking forlorn…her heart broken by her cold-hearted son… *Sniff…*"

"Hey, Wise! Stop narrating! God, you're so awful! Your personality sucks!"

"I don't think you should make Mama sad! I feel sorry for her!"

"Mm, mm, good girl, Porta. You're so nice. Well, taking Porta's opinion into account, I suppose I can grant you permission to stay, Mom."

"What the hell, Masato?! There's a pretty big discrepancy between how you treat the two of us!"

"That's based entirely on your relative humanity."

And they were bickering like always.

"Ms. Mamako! Do you mind?" a male student said, coming up to her. His face was all ASCII, so it was impossible to tell who he was, but he seemed earnest enough.

He bowed his head to Mamako, held out his hand, and with his heart on his sleeve, yelled, "Mamako! When I first saw you, I knew! Would you please…be my girlfriend?"

She was already being asked out.

Mamako handled it well, calmly smiling back at him.

"Thank you," she said. "I'm honored you feel that way... But I'm afraid I'm Ma-kun's mother, so I can't go out with you. I'm really sorry."

"I—I see... *Sniff...*"

The student ran away, furiously wiping at the fountain of tears.

Porta watched all this with astonishment. Wise furiously took notes.

"That's the sixth person to ask you out! You're amazing, Mama!"

"One more torpedoed. Counting written confessions, she's on her thirteenth... The commotion yesterday clearly skyrocketed her popularity. Now then, Masato, as her son, tell us, how do you feel about your mother's explosive popularity?"

"I wish I was dead. End of comment."

Who wanted to see boys their own age asking their mom out? Masato averted his eyes, feigning indifference.

But that left him facing the Cleric family. They were now sitting some distance from Masato's party...

"..." *Glaaare.*

The second Masato had looked their way, Medhimama fixed him with a fearsome scowl. It was unnerving, to say the least. "Urgh..." He hastily looked away, pretending he'd never looked that way at all.

"Ugh... I'm drawing a lot of aggro over here..."

"Well, duh. You blocked Medhi from making off with number one. And that old bat's being super competitive with Mamako to boot... Reckless idiot. No way she could ever beat Mamako. You know Mamako tops the Mom Rankings!"

"Wise, that's not true!" Mamako said, unusually stern for her. "There are no Mom Rankings. Your own mom is always number one. Everyone likes their own mom best. Even you, Wise."

"W-well... I mean...my mom's kinda a lost cause, but...I guess she is still my mom, so...maybe a part of me feels that way."

"See? I knew it. You agree, right, Porta?"

"Um, well... My mom is...the one I like best, I guess," Porta stammered. Was she just saying that to please Mamako?

"And of course, Ma-kun thinks I'm the best. Right?"

"Not at all. Last thing on my mind," he said.

Mamako looked very sad and started chanting her psychological debuff spell.

"...That's the worst thing anyone has ever said to me in all my life..." "Wait! Don't do that!" Every time she pulled that card, the hero bitterly regretted it. There was no defense against it. It wreaked havoc on his heart!

But this farce aside...

When he'd heard Mamako's speech, the first thing Masato thought was...

...Is that how Medhi feels?

Because she loved her mother, would she accept any awful treatment, believing firmly in her love?

Even though that awful treatment was making the dark emotions fester within her? Because it was her mother, she could stay with her?

Looking at Medhi sitting quietly beside her tyrant of a mother, Masato was only too aware he was sticking his nose in her business.

But before he could think on it further, Mr. Burly came in. "All right, Ma-kun. I'll be watching from the back!" "Yeah, yeah." Mamako retreated to the observation seats. Medhimama joined her but sat herself as far from Mamako as possible.

Morning homeroom started.

"Okay! Everyone's here. Well, morning news time!"

Mr. Burly turned toward the chalkboard, burly fingers clutching a thin piece of chalk.

And wrote...

School Festival.

"Today is the school festival! Let's all have a great time!"

"Yaaay! The school festival! ...Wait, whaaaaaaaaaaaaaaat?!"

"Mm? What's the matter, Hero Masato? Hardly seems worth the over-the-top reaction."

"No, this makes no sense! You can't have a surprise festival! That's nuts! Festivals are..."

"Normally you pick leaders, decide on a project, make preparations, and so on. Yes, that's all true! …However, the festival we're about to do is not merely a celebration but also a test to measure the student's ambition. Bear that in mind, if you would."

"Our…ambition?"

"How passionately are you able to throw yourself into an event that pops up out of nowhere? We'll evaluate your approach and grant points based on that. So, um…"

"Oh…I get it. Management would like us actively participating in events, then. I see. That is an urgent part of any game curriculum."

"Mm. If events are not exciting, then they not only failed to draw in new accounts but result in a number of recent and older accounts withdrawing. Success of events directly links to the longevity of a game. For the sake of this world, stop fussing and enjoy them. Now I'll explain the necessary conditions. Eyes up here."

Mr. Burly wished to protect the world he lived in.

On the board, he transcribed the key information for the in-game Gioco Accademia School Festival.

The festival would open that same day. It would take place in the morning and afternoon, and there was an evening event scheduled, too.

Students would join in the event as individuals or in parties, either attending or creating their own attractions. Whatever they wished.

"The school store will provide necessary materials. If you need significant equipment for things like stalls or plays, put in a request there. The school will take care of it. But there is a limit to the building data we can provide, and the locations available are first come, first served, so the key to victory is swift action. That's all from me! Don't sit this one out!"

And with that, Mr. Burly turned to leave.

"…Whoops, almost forgot," he added. "There's another special event tomorrow, so look forward to it!"

This time, Mr. Burly really did leave…

Nope, he's coming back again.

"Ah, sorry, sorry. There's one more thing I forgot. Since this is the school festival, parents and guardians are welcome to participate. This should make for some excellent memories to share with your children. That's all!"

"Huh? Wha…? Mr. Burly?! What are you…? Hey, don't leave!"

Masato tried to argue this last point, but Mr. Burly was gone in a flash. The bastard.

Morning homeroom ended. The classroom immediately grew quite loud. All students rose to their feet, discussing party formations and festival plans with their friends, everyone getting very worked up. They had an hour to get ready. Time was of the essence.

Masato's party was off to a great start… Well, not really. Masato was clutching his head in agony. Again.

"Even the festivals have moms involved… Why…? What's this school even for…?"

"At this point, you just need to accept what fate has in store for you… Anyway, if you've got time to grumble about it, then you better start thinking about what we should do. We've got no time."

"Yes… Oh, I know, Ma-kun! What about a stall? I'm a pretty good cook, if I do say so myself."

"Oh, sounds great. I'm in."

"Me too! I want to run a shop with Mama!"

"…Mom's not only part of the discussion; she's steering the whole thing… Why…? What's the point…?"

Masato dug his fingers deeper into his hair, groaning all the while.

"If I may," Medhimama said.

She and Medhi had come over to them.

"I happened to overhear you discussing plans for a stall. In which case…"

Medhimama snapped her finger out, pointing directly at Mamako.

"Let's have a contest! The victor decided by which stall ends up selling more!"

"Huh? …Um… Okay…?"

Mamako halfheartedly activated a mom-off!
Mamako herself didn't really seem to get it, but Medhimama was full speed ahead!

"...*Sigh*... Gawd... This toxic bitch is so obnoxious..."

Medhi's gloomy snarl was not lost on Masato.

Medhimama's forceful enthusiasm was really distracting, but Masato's attention was focused on Medhi's—"We will emerge victorious! Grrrrr!" Wow, Medhimama, shut up already. What was wrong with her? She was just exhausting.

The school provided the major equipment needed for stalls, but there were only so many available on a first come, first served basis.

Speed was vital, yet they'd wasted a bunch of time dealing with a loudmouthed old bat and submitted their application late. The result...

The setup Masato's party received was a stall designed to look like a diner in a rustic town.

"It's kinda like...some shop that shut down years ago."

"More like one that's technically still operating, but you've never seen anyone actually go in."

"Um... I-it does look a little old!"

"Mommy thinks it looks cozy and relaxing."

Their descriptions varied, but all agreed it was run-down. A shop that had clearly seen better days.

Running things out of a shop like this was just depressing... But wait, it wasn't all bad news.

The building itself was unfortunate, but the one saving grace was the location. The party's shop was built along the main road leading from the school gate to the school building. Everyone visiting the festival would walk past them. They'd scored a high-traffic area, and that was worth celebrating...

Or maybe not, given their surroundings.

"My, my, my. What a filthy hovel! You poor things."

An obnoxious laugh filled the air. The owner of the stall directly across from them, Medhimama, had come to scope them out, Medhi in tow.

They had the sort of fancy café you'd find in the heart of any major metropolis. An artistically engineered design fitted with natural-looking fake plants, all excessively polished with a sun-drenched wooden patio out front.

"Ugh... How is theirs so much better...?"

"Ohhh-ho-ho-ho! It looks like our victory is guaranteed before we've even begun! Customers will flock to our stall in droves! You'll be left twiddling your thumbs, watching them forlornly! Ohhh-ho-ho-ho-ho!"

Having delivered this final blow, Medhimama withdrew into her shop.

But the moment she turned her back on them, Medhi came over, bowing her head apologetically.

"Sorry, Masato. She can be so rude..."

"Uh, oh, don't worry about it," Masato said. "You don't need to apologize for her. We're cool."

Reassured, she turned to leave.

"Oh, wait... Hey, Medhi," Masato said, stopping her. There was something bothering him.

"Yes? What is it?"

"About yesterday. Outside, after the pool class...you sort of went, uh...berserk? That's what it looked like to me anyway... Is that...?"

Masato wasn't really sure how to ask this.

Medhi flinched. For the tiniest moment, he saw a tense look on her face.

Then, "Oh? I don't know what you mean."

She gave him an adorable little head tilt. Like she genuinely had no idea what he was talking about. "I need to get back, though. Good luck!" "Oh, um..." But Medhi was already gone.

Did she just run away? It sure felt like it...but well, neither one of them were comfortable discussing the subject openly, so maybe he should leave her alone for now. It really bothered him, but maybe best not to push things.

They had to get the shop ready anyway.

Masato put that all behind him and stared at their pitiful stall.

"What do we do about this...?" he asked.

"Dunno if there's anything we can do," Wise said. "We're gonna be operating out of a real dive. Nothing we can do about it, so we just gotta make the best of it."

"Yes! We just have to make this the best dive we can! ...It doesn't matter how old the shop looks! What matters is how we treat customers!"

"Porta, you're so right. Customer service is everything. So, Ma-kun..."

"Yeah, I get it. Just gotta make the best of it. All of us, together."

Together.

The very idea threatened to plunge him into despair. He struggled to keep his head up.

...But Mom's involved...

That thought kept coming back to smack him again, but he did his best to force it out of his brain. To empty his mind.

The party went inside to start getting ready.

The interior was as shabby as the exterior. Cheap tables and chairs, a messy, dirty-looking kitchen behind the counter. Everything was dimly lit and run-down. This was what they had to work with.

"We don't have much time, so let's split the tasks up. As far as the food we're gonna serve, Mom's the best cook, so we'll leave it all up to you. Let us know what you need."

"Got it. Leave it to Mommy!"

"And if we need anything, let's have Porta make them. Plates and whatever else. Is that okay with you, Porta?"

"Yes! I've got you covered!"

"So Wise and I will have to clean the place. Nothing we can do about how shabby it is, but let's at least make it sanitary."

"Yeah, yeah, I figured. It's a chore, but it's gotta get done. I dunno if cleaning this mess will really make much of a difference, though..."

"Fair... Just thought I'd like to try to brighten the place up somehow. If we can at least make it a little less gloomy-looking..."

The shop was downright claustrophobic. Masato looked around, searching for inspiration.

"Oh, I know! I have an idea!" Mamako said.

Everyone looked at her. "Wise, lend me your ear." "Mm? What?" She whispered to Wise for a minute. Masato couldn't make out what she was saying.

Wise pulled out her magic tome and began chanting a spell.

"...*Spara la magia per mirare... Bomba Sfera!* And! *Bomba Sfera!*"

Wise activated chain cast. Two exploding spheres appeared.

Each hit a wall. *Ka-boooooooooooooooooooooom.* The walls were totally blown away.

Much better. Great view of the outside... Wait.

"What?! Wise, what the hell?!"

"I just did what Mamako told me to do."

"She told you to...? Mom! What were you thinking?!"

"Now we've got some outside light coming in, and there's a lovely breeze!"

"Yeah, sure, but... Argh! We're drawing a crowd! And everyone can see inside!"

A number of students were gathering outside the shop, drawn by the sound of the explosion. Who could blame them? They were peering into the shop, making Masato feel like he was in a zoo...

And then Mamako did it again.

"Oh, I know! Mommy has another idea!"

"Nope. We've had enough ideas outta you. Please just don't do anything else."

"Oh, don't say that. Hear me out first, okay? You see..." Mamako took Masato's arm, leaning over, and whispered in his ear.

When he heard her idea, Masato...

"............................Huh?"

...was so stunned it was all he could do to blink at her.

He genuinely, completely, from the bottom of his heart had no idea what to say.

The festival was about to start. He didn't have time to think it over.

The announcer's voice echoed through the school grounds.

"Your attention, please! The first annual Gioco Accademia School Festival begins…now!"

This signaled both the opening of the festival and the start of the fight.

When she heard the announcement, a smug smile spread across Medhimama's lips.

"It begins," she said.

She was in the owner's office on the second floor of her fancy café.

Lounging on a couch, elegantly filing her nails, passing the time in comfort. And utter confidence.

Naturally. She'd already done all there was to do. Her plans were flawless.

"The shop itself is perfect. Our location is ideal. The sweets and drinks we're serving are top-class items purchased at the finest shop in town. And more than anything, the most beautiful student in class, my daughter, is our waitress. We will be outdone on nothing!"

Indeed. They would not lose. Victory was the only outcome. This was a battle they were destined to win. Perhaps that was a little dull, but nonetheless, she felt fantastic.

"Now then, I should go take a look. As the owner, I must say hello from time to time. Ohhh-ho-ho-ho. I imagine I'll be showered with compliments."

The festival had only just begun, but she was sure the shop would be packed with customers. How could it not be?

She hoped she would have enough room to walk through the crowd.

Medhimama went downstairs and found…

"…Huh?"

…the shop was completely empty. The fancy luxury chairs and tables were all lined up with no one sitting in them. "How? How?

How?!" She looked again, and again, but there were zero customers here.

"Th-this isn't..."

The shocking sight made her dizzy, and she swayed, but she managed to stay on her feet.

What was going on here? She wanted to start screaming but controlled herself.

"R-right. The festival's only just begun. Perhaps it's too soon to start getting upset."

Yes. That must be it. She'd come to check on things too quickly. The gates had only just opened, and the guests hadn't made it this far back yet. What else?

Medhimama told herself all this and settled down at a table. Making it *look* like she was a customer... Actually, no, not really. She simply wished to observe.

Then the shop door opened. The shop's very first customer! Medhimama hopped to her feet... No, that wasn't it.

"I'm back."

At the door was Medhi, wearing a waitress outfit. Dressed beautifully, in an outfit that would surely defeat all competition, she moved with elegance, bowing politely to the shop interior.

She noticed her mother sitting there.

"Oh, Mother. What brings you here?"

"O-oh, just checking in. Where did you go?"

"I went to scope out Masato's shop."

"Oh, really? It seems like the festival hasn't drawn much of a crowd yet, and even if it did, hardly anyone would visit *that* shop. I don't see what good scouting them would..."

"No, that's not true at all. It is still early, but their shop is packed."

"...Huh?"

Medhimama couldn't believe her ears. Packed?

No. No, no, no, no. That couldn't be. It made no sense. How could that be?

But...but if it was true...

"Don't be ridiculous! There's no way they..." Medhimama said, flying out the door. "Wha...?!" she gasped, unable to believe her eyes.

Across the street...were a hundred people lined up to eat at a diner. Above the door was a sign that read MOTHER'S BACK.

Masato and Wise had their hands full dealing with the crowd. They were getting desperate.

"Excuse me! Please don't block the entrance! Form an orderly line! Please!"

"Anyone who doesn't listen will get a lecture from Mamako... Wait, no, that's just a reward for these... J-just line up like we say! Keep the doors clear! Being able to see inside the shop from the street is, like, one of the shop's selling points!"

The crowd proved fairly obedient, forming a neat line. What well-mannered NPCs. Definitely made in Japan. Cultures that habitually form lines never forget to program that behavior.

Now everyone passing could see inside.

The Mother's Back diner had a see-through design, with no walls on either side.

The seats inside the shop were lined up like a classroom, with all diners facing the same direction. All seats were already full.

All the diners' eyes were on the kitchen, and Mamako inside.

She was chopping vegetables on a cutting board, keeping an eye on the pot on the stove.

Masato had grown up seeing her like this. Watching his mother's back as she got dinner ready.

Every now and then she'd turn around, smile, and speak to the crowd.

"It's almost ready, so you all be good little boys and girls and wait just a little longer!"

Yep, there'd been many a day she spoke to him like that. And naturally...

""""Okaaay! We'll waaaait!""""" the diners replied with gusto.

Their actual ages had no bearing. All the diners were children to her. And as children, manners dictated that they draw out the vowels. It was an iron-clad rule.

Advanced diners managed to add a note of petulant exasperation to it that was extremely toddler-like.

Mother's Back was a concept diner that revolved around the idea of mom cooking for you. It had proven extremely popular with oversized children everywhere.

They were so busy that Masato and Wise were already worn-out.

"*Sigh...* This is already a mess."

"Y-yeah... I always thought all boys had a bit of an Oedipus complex, but I didn't think it would be this effective... This is nuts..."

"Mom's idea paid off... Argh... I'm glad the shop's doing well, but I'm suuuper not comfortable with this at the same time..."

"Ohhh, I get it. You're her kid, so you don't like having Mamako be everybody's mom. She's making you *jealous. Pfft.*"

"She is not! That's not it!"

"Heh-heh-heh, so you say, but deep down..."

"Um, Masato! Wise!" Porta called, scurrying around. "If you're done wrangling the line, could you please come help? I can't handle all this myself!"

"Whoops, our star server's starting to panic. Better go rescue her."

Masato didn't have time to deny Wise's teasing now. Porta had been left to take all the orders herself. He quickly went to help.

He filled a bunch of water glasses, put them on a tray, and started passing them out. "Still need water here!" "Oh, yeah, coming right up!" "Can I get a refill?" "Sure! On my way!" He was soon running back and forth.

Then the food started coming out, and he had to deliver that.

"Ready! Mommy's special omelet rice. Can you take it out?"

"Got it! ...Um, what table ordered that...?"

"Yo, hurry that up! Mom's food is getting cold!"

"R-right! On my way! ...Sorry to keep you waiting!"

"Wait, this isn't right! I didn't order this!"

"What?! S-s-sorry!"

Argh, already so busy his eyes were spinning. And the harder he worked, the more people got mad at him. What the hell? He was ready to cry.

He looked around for help, but Mamako was focused on cooking, and Porta and Wise were being run as ragged as Masato, so there was no one else to pick up the slack. They needed more hands.

Just then…

"Oh, I know! Mommy just had a good idea."

"Another one? What now…?"

"Hee-hee. Leave this to Mommy!"

Mamako called out to the diners.

"Are there any good little boys or girls who want to help Mommy out? I'd just love it if you gave me a hand."

We're busy, so help us. She was straight up asking the customers to help. "Hey! Mom!" That seemed like poor form. They'd never go for something like… They did.

"Oh, I'll help! I'm helping Mooommmy!"

"H-hey, wait! *I'm* gonna help Mommy! I'll pass out chopsticks!"

"Hee-hee. You're such good children! Thank you!"

The children were thrilled to help.

"I—I want to help, too! I'll help serve the food! Oh, Hero Masato. Can I take that tray from you?"

"Um, sure, thanks… Wait, Mr. Burly?"

Including one very familiar diner, the children clamored to help Mom out, snatching the work away from the servers.

Masato's party had nothing left to do. The three of them stood there, looking at the crowd of overgrown children.

"…Masato, you know what I'm thinking?"

"Yeah, probably. But let's not say it aloud. They are our customers."

"I—I think they're all really nice! That's all!"

Porta was right. It was definitely not appropriate to call them creepy.

Nice was a much better word for it.

*　　*　　*

At the entrance to Mother's Back, someone was peering inside.

Medhimama. Medhi by her side.

"*Tch*, why? What is going on? How is it so popular?"

"Um, Mother," Medhi said, anxious, "everyone's looking at us. I don't think we should peep like..."

"You be quiet! They'll notice us!" Medhimama brushed her off, biting her nails. This was mortifying.

She looked back at her own shop. They had no customers at all, just the sound of crickets. It was enough to make her want to cry.

The difference was clear. At this rate, she was going to lose. She had to do something.

"...Oh, I know. I know just the thing."

Medhimama's smile turned sinister, and she raised her staff.

Suddenly...

"Augh! What the...?!"

A cry rang out over the bustle of Mamako's children.

"What? What's wrong?" Masato said, hurrying over. He did work here, after all.

There was a Mysterious Object X sitting in front of a male customer, all blobby and slimy and brownish, reddish purple.

"Whoa... What *is* that...?"

"That's what I wanna know! I was about to eat, and it turned into this! Are you serving this to customers? ...I oughta sue! You owe me damages for this! I demand compensation! It's the least you can do for me, right?"

"U-um, well..."

"How much can you pay me right now? I mean, I might just spread word about this around. And you don't want that, do you? Huh?"

This customer had quickly turned from a child into a blackmailer. What now?

Then Mamako heard the commotion and came flying out of the kitchen. She ran over to the angry customer and started bowing her head.

"Oh my goodness! I'm so sorry! I can't believe this happened!"

Mamako bowed her head again and again, apologizing desperately.

In the process, her supersize portions began bouncing up and down. "Whoa... W-wow..." The man opened his mouth to complain, but his eyes were glued to her chest...

And a diner nearby muttered, "Hey, wait... Is this part of the show? If you're lucky enough to get a failed dish, Mommy Mamako will show up with some extra-jiggly dessert?"

"Mommy jiggle... How avant-garde! That stimulates my pioneering soul! And I do mean *stimulates*!"

"I must blaze this new trail! Give me another dish! Let it be a failure, please!"

Well, that was one way to interpret events. And one way to react to them.

The would-be blackmailer found himself the target of a number of envious glares.

"I-I'm not angry!" he said, going back to the good-boy routine. "I could never be mad at you!"

He took a firm grip on his spoon and with a blissful smile began eating the Mysterious Object X. "Oh, yummy! It looks weird, but it tastes great!" Apparently, the food only looked weird. As weird as this dude's mind.

The tension in the shop dissipated, reverting to the original mood, with Mamako cooking and the children happily helping. With the customers ordering extra helpings, hoping to hit the jackpot, sales actually improved. Business was booming.

Masato watched for a few minutes, then went back to where Wise and Porta were sitting, eating their own meals.

"Nice one, Masato!"

"Masato, well done!"

"Thanks, thanks. But all I did was get yelled at. Mom ended up handling it for me again. Problem is..."

"Yep, that was definitely sabotage."

"I think she used magic to change what the food looked like! I'm so mad!"

"Yep... Should we say something?"

To stop this from getting any worse, it might be better to handle it quickly. As much as he wanted a rest, Masato turned and headed out of the shop.

Outside...

"Ngggh! Th-this calls for my last resort! Medhi!"

"Yes, Mother."

"Go change into your swimsuit! Then burst into Mamako's shop in your swimsuit and do a sexy dance in front of her customers! Quickly!"

"Yes, Moth— No, wait. Why do I have to...?!"

"You in a swimsuit will be the bait to lure them into my shop! You're the most beautiful girl here, and there's no way they'll be able to resist you! If you insist, I'll even allow you to do *that* suggestive pose."

"I wasn't even going to *ask* for that!"

"Oh, stop griping and do what I say! This is an order!"

"B-but..."

When Medhimama got this competitive, she thought nothing of forcing Medhi into impossible tasks.

Even for the sake of victory, demanding racy moves from your daughter was hardly appropriate. In fact, it was extremely inappropriate. It wasn't that Masato was opposed to seeing that...but he figured he should probably step in.

Trying not to add fuel to the fire (likely an impossible task), Masato spoke softly.

"Um, thanks for stopping by! But we do ask that you refrain from creating a fuss outside the shop."

"What?! This hardly qualifies as a fuss! Enough with your baseless accusations!"

Medhimama reacted like a rabid dog.

But when she realized it was Masato, her attitude changed immediately. She puffed herself up, trying to act like everything was going great. Pride really is something.

"O-oh, Masato. How aaare you? Fancy meeting you here."

"Where else would I be? I'm fine, though, thanks for asking."

"So? What do you want?"

"Um, well... About that... You see..."

Face-to-face, it was hard to directly voice his complaint. Even though he was in the right, actually saying it out loud wasn't easy. He considered dropping it entirely.

Behind him, Wise called, "Say it!" She gave him a push. "Masato! Do your best!" Porta cried, earnestly cheering him on.

And Medhi was watching him closely. Like she wanted his help.

This was not a battle he could pull out of.

"...Um, Medhimama," Masato began, "I think that's about enough."

"Enough? Enough of what?"

"Everything. Competitions, making Medhi to do the impossible... I really wish you'd drop all of it. Please."

Masato bowed his head, making it a request. Earnestly, seriously, fervently pleading with her.

"Never," Medhimama snapped. "Competitions are no game. Once entered, you must tackle them with all your might and continue doing so until victory is decided. Dropping out partway is out of the question. There's no point unless a clear victor is decided."

"I think the victor is already pretty obvious... Just look at our relative customer counts."

"Th-this contest isn't decided by which shop is more popular! That's just... That's a problem with the shop! Nothing to do with us! Not a problem for us at all!"

"But the contest is decided by who sells the most..."

"Shut up! The point is! We should be competing in a more direct fashion! Receive public evaluations by a number of people, find some way to make victory clear, make this contest fair and square! That would be better for everyone!"

"Ehhhh..."

They'd clearly be evaluated enough. And look who was complaining about fair and square. Masato was too disgusted to bother pointing it out, though.

Just then...

"Your attention, please!" called a student walking nearby. "I'm a festival admin. It's time for the beauty contest! Participants needed! Nominate yourself or another—we don't care!"

Speak of the devil. "You there!" "Eeek!" Medhimama pounced on them.

"You said something about a beauty contest? Is that true?!" *Grrr.*

"Y-yes! Recruiting entrants now! Open to all! Even as an advertisement for your stall! Come on and join!"

"Then Medhi will be representing our stall! Masato, put someone from your stall up, too! We'll have a contest between our shops' star staff!"

"No, wait, you can't just decide that for—!" Masato tried to stop her, but...

"Fine," Wise said, popping up out of nowhere. "Let's do this! Let's find out who has the best waitress!"

You could search the whole world over and find no one else who thought Wise was their stall's star waitress.

But if she wanted to do this, why not let her?

The beauty contest was held in the special hall set up on the school grounds.

The student serving as MC grabbed the mic with a flourish, calling out to the gathered crowd.

"Thank you for waiting! The main event of this school festival, the school beauty contest, is about to begin! Put your hands together!"

"Yay!" "Come on!" "Get started!" "We're here for the girls, not you!" The crowd was vocal and excited. And quite large.

"It's gonna be extra painful when Wise self-destructs here... Poor girl."

"I—I hope she doesn't! I think she deserves number one!"

"What nonsense. Medhi will clearly emerge victorious. Oh-ho-ho!"

Medhimama certainly seemed confident, but well, she was probably justified in that. Masato offered up a silent prayer for Wise... *At least make it quick. Don't let Wise suffer. If that's even possible.*

So.

"First, I'll explain how this contest will be scored. This beauty contest is not decided by a panel of judges or by formal voting but by the volume of the audience's response! Maybe some of you are thinking, 'By the volume? Isn't that a little subjective?' But don't worry! We have specialized equipment to measure the volume accurately! Look here!"

The backstage staff pushed a cart out onto the stage.

It had a large panel on it labeled CHEER MEASURING DEVICE.

"The volume measured will be displayed digitally on this panel! Measurements will be in decibels, and that number will be the entrant's score! Their rankings will be decided by volume alone! Which means...you guessed it! Even if only one person supports them, if they cheer loud enough, they might push their choice to victory! Isn't that a lovely system?"

Scores in decibels. Maybe that was a good idea. Much better than everything being decided on the whim of some judges anyway.

On the other hand, if the audience didn't have your back, nobody would cheer at all. You'd be left standing forlornly in front of a silent crowd. He wasn't saying who, but he already felt sorry for her.

But with that, they were starting.

"Well, let's introduce the lovely ladies who have entered! Entry number one...Medhi, the Cleric! Come on out!"

"Okay! Thank you very much!" Medhi said, sounding a little nervous.

She came running out onstage, wearing her waitress uniform. Hugging a menu tightly to her magnificent chest, her frills all flouncing. The audience was already buzzing.

Once Medhi reached the center of the stage, she bowed before the mic stand…

…a little too hastily. She bopped her head on the mic.

"Ow… S-sorry! Oooh…that's so embarrassing…"

Medhi turned bright red all the way to her ears. She hid her face behind the menu. A moment later…

""""""C-cuuuuuuuuuuuuuuute!"""""""

An explosion of *moe* raced across the crowd. It was deafening.

The volume was measured, and the score lit up. Ninety decibels.

The same volume as a bulldozer from five yards away. Unbearably loud.

"Whoa! Kicking things off with a huge score! The Cleric Medhi is very popular!"

"Th-thank you! Thank you very much! Um… I'm working at a café on the main street! I hope to see you all there! I'll be waiting! Pardon me!"

Medhi was too embarrassed to stay put. She rattled off at top speed and beat a hasty retreat toward the back of the stage…but stumbled along the way. The crowd seemed even more enthusiastic about this.

Seeing her daughter showered with cheers definitely put her mother in a good mood. "Well done, Medhi! Flawless! Victory is yours!" Like she'd already won.

The MC seemed to be getting worked up himself.

"Well, she was certainly a wonderfully clumsy waitress! Thank you very much! Moving right along! Entry number two, come on out!"

"Thanks! I'm class president number two! I'm an NPC student, so I don't have a name! But most everyone else is the same, so I don't really care!"

She got a laugh with this self-deprecating remark, and with that, a parade of entrants came through.

They were all NPC students, with hastily slapped together ASCII faces, which made it tough to call any of them cute, exactly…but there were, like, seven of them.

The NPC entrances all got between fifty decibels (the volume of an exhaust fan from a yard away) to seventy decibels (the volume of a cicada from two yards away). Not bad, considering.

And at last, after all that buildup, it was her turn.

"Well, that sure was exciting! Let's keep the party going! Entry number nine! The Sage Wise! Come on out!"

"Ha-ha! At last, time for the victor to shine!"

Here we go. The self-destruction expert, here to show us how it's done. Masato clapped quietly, keeping his eyes peeled.

Wise came out in her usual outfit, an apron over it. She skipped to the center of the stage.

And when she bowed before the mic, she hit her head on it.

"Yowch! Aw, sorry! I'm such a klutz! Tee-hee!"

I'm not even kidding. She actually did that.

The result…

""""…………………………*Sigh…*"""""

The entire audience sighed in unison.

The volume measured was only twenty decibels. The same as leaves rustling in a breeze. That's it.

Porta was doing her best to cheer for Wise all by herself. "Yaaay! Wiiiise!" But Masato quietly reached out and stopped her. She was just making it worse.

Masato's heart ached for his fallen companion, but Medhimama was delighted.

"Well, that clinches it," she murmured. "Ohhh-ho-ho-ho!"

"Yeah, it does. I can't argue that."

At the very least, Wise's defeat didn't seem to have caused a stir. The contest hall was dead quiet.

The only noise was up onstage.

"Huh?! What's with that reaction? You all liked it when Medhi did it! You like this sort of crap, right? Why aren't you cheering?"

"Thank you very much, Sage Wise. Please go away now."

"Hold up, even the MC is acting bored?! And that last bit was rude!"

Wise was chased off to the end of the row of entrants at the back of the stage.

The MC took a beat to recover and turned to continue.

"Um… I'd love to try to recover the mood by introducing our next contestant, but…we actually only had these nine entrants, so… that's all there is…"

He bowed apologetically to a chorus of boos. "What? You're kidding!" "We can't end like that!" "You can't end on a downer!" Anger raged. Wise had left a bad taste in everyone's mouth. People were ready to riot.

The MC desperately tried to placate the crowd, saying, "I know! I feel the same way! We can't let it end like this! Which means…we're calling for last-minute entrants! Don't care if you nominate yourself or someone else! Just come on up to the stage! Please!"

"Oh, then I don't mind if I do!"

You already know who responded. It was Mamako.

The moment he realized this, Masato buried his head in his knees. There was no way this could possibly end well from his perspective.

Mamako was wearing an apron and holding a pot with both hands. She carried it up the stairs at the side of the stage and went over to Wise.

"Er, um, Mamako? …What's up?"

"Well, I didn't have enough burners at the shop, so I couldn't warm up the miso soup. So I thought I'd ask you to use your fire magic. Do you mind?"

"Oh, um, sure. That's easy enough. But…if you're here, who's in the shop?"

"We don't need to worry about that! Shiraaase came to check in on us, and she agreed to watch it for us. Shiraaase's a mom, too, so it's okay."

Masato pictured a nun in an apron standing in the kitchen, totally calm, saying, "Let me infooorm you that your food will soon be ready."

"Are you kidding?! She'll destroy the place! You'd better get back before the shop closes down for good!"

Wise quickly chanted a spell, Fuoco Fiamma, generating a flame on her hand. "Thanks, that's such a help!" Mamako said, holding the pot over the flame. They stood there a minute.

The miso soup was soon simmering.

"Well? That seem about right?"

"Yes, thank you. I appreciate it. Now, then… Oh, look, there's a microphone! I should at least plug our shop!"

Holding the piping-hot soup pot to one side, Mamako leaned into the mic.

"Hello, everyone! The miso soup is ready! It's really hot, so I'll make sure to blow on it for you! Come have some!"

Instantly…

""""YEEEEEEEEEEEEEEEEEEEEEAHHHH! A girl who can cook? So cuuuuuuuuuuuuuuuuuuuuuuuuute!"""""

The audience was downright bellowing. The noise shook the earth.

She was hardly of an age where you'd call her a "girl" or "cute," but with her baby face, everyone just assumed Mamako was a student here.

The number on the panel showed 120 decibels. Like standing near a jet engine. A volume that could cause hearing damage.

The MC saw these results and announced, "Wow, that decides it! It's all over, folks! The victor is Mamako! Congratulations!"

"O-oh?"

The winner of the beauty contest was Mamako. She was officially Miss Gioco Accademia.

She was a Mrs., not a Miss, but oh well.

The shocking last-minute twist had left Medhimama practically catatonic.

And the festival itself drew to a close…

It was evening. The group stood by the gates of the school.

The festival had ended, and the students were headed home.

"Arghhhh! …I can't believe it! What the hell?! This is ridiculous!"

Medhimama was ranting like a woman possessed. She slammed

her staff into the ground. The gem shattered, and the staff broke in two.

Mom-only gear was surprisingly fragile. Or was she just that mad? Either way, this did not exactly calm her down.

"I refuse to accept it! This can't be happening! We can't seem to win at all! It doesn't make any sense!"

"Mother! Please calm down! We..."

"Shut up!"

"Eek!"

Medhi tried to control her mother, but Medhimama grabbed her daughter's arm and yanked her forward, scowling furiously at her.

"M-Mother...?"

"That's right... That's it, Medhi. The source of all our problems is you, isn't it? You didn't become number one like you were supposed to! That's the cause! If you would just win, then we wouldn't have had any problems! Why didn't you?!"

"I...I do apologize for my poor results in class, but..."

"I don't care about any lip service apology! What are you going to do about it? How are you going to fix this? Tell me, Medhi! How are you going to make things right?!"

"I—I don't know... I don't know what to..."

"You brought this mess on us, and you don't even know how to fix it? Unbelievable! That's enough! You're worthless! You must be punished!"

Medhimama raised her hand. Palm ready to strike Medhi's cheek.

Masato wasn't about to let that happen again.

"Wait!" he said, reaching out and grabbing Medhimama's arms. "You're just disgracing yourself."

Bloodshot eyes turned on Masato. He stood firm. He wasn't going to back down here.

Frankly, he was the one about to lose it, but he fought off his anger, forcing himself to stay calm and meet Medhimama's eyes. Calmly.

"Please stop doing this."

"Mind your own business! This is between me and my daughter! It has nothing to do with you!"

"How so? You've gotten us mixed up in your mess at every turn. Knock it off already. Let's all just calm down here. Everyone's staring."

"Who's staring...?!"

They were surrounded by students on their way home, many of whom had stopped to watch. Wise, Porta, and Mamako were all watching anxiously.

Mamako's gaze most likely had the biggest effect. Medhimama likely didn't want to look any more pathetic than she already did. She quieted down considerably, pulling herself out of Masato's grasp and turning her back on him.

He'd stopped her for now. But what next?

Masato glanced toward his party. Wise and Porta, sure, but even Mamako didn't seem to know what to do. They were all just staring back at him.

Then...

...*Mm?*

Masato felt a chill run down his spine. Like something really dangerous was coming closer. And the source of that chill...was right next to him.

He glanced that way.

"...*Gonna kill her...*"

There was something there. Something cloaked in an aura of darkness. Something staring at the back of Medhimama's head with a crazed gleam in her eyes, raising a staff high above her head.

It was Medhi. Inches from pummeling Medhimama.

"Yiiiiiikes! Stop! Time-oooooout!"

Masato quickly pinned Dark Medhi's arms behind her back. Part of him definitely wanted to let her get a hit in, but not like this. This could only end badly.

"Eeek! M-Masato?!"

Medhi turned around, looking just as she always did. The dark power had vanished in an instant. Her face was so close to his, he instinctively bent backward. It was just as beautiful as ever.

"Um, what's going on?"

"What's going on? That's what I wanna know! You were downright terrifying there!"

"I was? ...I can't seem to recall anything like that, though..."

Medhi's unmistakably beautiful face tilted to one side, baffled. How could she not remember...? It was like she was desperately feigning innocence. What was he going to do with her? What *could* he do?

Either way, he couldn't keep pinning her arms, his body pressed up against hers. It was not good for his mental health. He was a little unsure if it was safe to release her, but he slowly did.

And just as this side of things settled down, the even more problematic half started moving again. Not giving him a chance to breathe.

"What is all that fuss? Quit your muttering! *Sigh...*"

Medhimama had definitely calmed down a lot, but he wasn't letting his guard down yet. Masato quietly placed Medhi behind him, standing between the two, not letting either go after the other.

Medhimama looked Masato over and let out another deep sigh.

"...I won't raise a hand to her."

"Sorry, but I can't just take your word for it. Either of yours."

"Either? ...I don't know what you mean by that, but fine. Take Medhi with you. Medhi would probably like that better."

"No. I'm going with you, Mother."

Medhi stepped out from behind Masato's protection, placing herself next to Medhimama.

Medhimama looked at her with genuine surprise.

"...You're sure?"

"Yes. I want to be with you, Mother. If you'll allow it."

"No, wait, Medhi, if the two of you are alone together..."

You'll hit her. He wasn't sure if he should say that. He wanted to but couldn't quite bring himself to.

Medhi shook her head slightly. "Don't worry. I promise," she said softly. Was that a promise not to hit her mom? He was super unsure how much he could trust her right now.

"Mother. Do you mind if I stay with you?"

"...Do what you like. The inn we were staying at kicked us out because of...some nonsense about another reservation. We'll have to find a new place to stay. Best to get that sorted out quickly. If you're coming with me, do so at once."

"Yes, Mother."

The Cleric family went away, the daughter following on the mother's heels.

Talking quietly to each other.

"...I should apologize."

"No need, Mother. I understand. You're always thinking of what's best for me, and that makes you strict sometimes. I know that."

"Yes... You're a very good girl."

Medhi smiled. Medhimama looked uncomfortable but managed to smile back.

It looked like they'd made a kind of peace.

The whole incident still preying on his mind, Masato watched them walk away.

That evening, in the inn's baths...

"*Sigh...* I just don't know..."

...a drop of water fell from the ceiling, hitting him on the forehead. Masato was lost in thought.

The hot water was draining the fatigue of the festival away, and he was giving his limbs a light massage.

What was he thinking about? What else?

"Whew... It's a little on the hot side but quite nice! Baths the whole family can use are something else."

The foremost problem in his mind: Why was Mamako sitting next to him?

He glanced in her direction, and yep, it was still her next to him. Treasured chest island ×2 floating on the surface of the water, thoroughly enjoying sharing the bath with her son. Her skin flushed a pale pink.

And it wasn't just her.

"Geez... Why does this always happen? It ain't right..."

"It's a bit hot, but I can handle it! It's fun to take a bath with everyone!"

Wise and Porta were here, too, beyond the steam rising off the water.

Wise was in maximum defensive mode. She had everything from the nose down below the water and had been muttering to herself the entire time, ready to commit murder at the slightest excuse.

Porta seemed to be happily enjoying the water. Her precious bag was on her head, never leaving her body. Such a good kid.

Suddenly, a surprise fanfare played in Masato's head.

Masato's secret title, Mixed Bath Creep Level 1, advanced to Mixed Bath Creep Level 2! Well done!

So, well, the first thing on Masato's mind was definitely this state of affairs.

"...Why...why is this happening...?"

"Because you walked straight into the girls' bath, you freak."

"I did not! When I went in, the curtains were definitely for the men's bath! And while I was in here, I guess it became women's hours. But you saw I was in here, and you all still chose to join me! Who's the shameless one here?"

"I didn't want to! But these two...!"

"I don't see what the problem is. Everyone bathing together is a good thing!"

"Yes! Bathing with your party is nice!"

"And then they start talking like this! If I refuse, it's like I hate them or something! I had no choice!"

And thus, this situation had everyone's explicit consent. He was safe...right?

Well.

"Well, now that everyone's settled down," Mamako began, "it's time for the customary naked strategy session! Yay!"

"Wh-when did that become customary?"

"You know what they say! Bare your body and soul, and don't ever hide what you're thinking. It's so important! So...Ma-kun? There's something you want to share with everyone, isn't there? Mommy can tell just by looking at you. What's the problem of the day?"

"Well, obviously… Medhi and her mother."

""""…Ohhh…"""""

Everyone hung their heads. No need to explain it. Everyone had witnessed the same things and knew exactly what was going on. The same thought floated into everyone's minds.

Wise gave an exasperated sigh. "You know what I think? I think we oughta just leave them to it."

"We can't just do that, though. If something isn't done, they'll seriously…"

"Yeah, maybe. But the old bat treats her daughter and everyone around like trash, and she won't hear a word of protest from anyone. And Medhi's being Medhi and dutifully following the hag around. Nowhere for us to butt in."

"Yeah, but…I don't think Medhimama can go on like that, and Medhi's stress levels are only gonna get worse. If the darkness inside her continues to grow…"

"I can totally see a healer running a Darkness build. Drain-type spells that siphon HP and MP are usually Dark, so if she focuses on spells like that, she'd actually be pretty useful."

"That's not the problem…"

"Then what is? I mean, Masato, why should you even care about either of them?"

"Well…"

Now that she mentioned it, Masato didn't really have a legitimate reason to be this focused on the problems of Medhi and her mother. It wasn't his job. It wasn't necessary.

As a hero, it was his duty to tighten his bonds to his own mother, but even that responsibility was one forced on him during account creation.

But even so, Masato thought…

"…I can't just ignore them. Or at least, I don't want to. I can't just call it someone else's problem."

Masato saw his own problems in their problems. Medhi's position and feelings hit painfully close to home.

A mother whose behavior restricted her kid's behavior, putting pressure on them. Rebellious feelings festering inside. He'd worked through all of that. He was well aware of just how hard it could be.

He'd thought he'd finally met his ideal heroine, and the glimpses of the darkness within her felt like a betrayal of that ideal and left him feeling powerless to help. Even so...

"I just feel like there must be something I can do. But I need your help to do it. Please."

Masato bowed his head, asking for his party's help.

"Mommy agrees," Mamako said, her warm voice a great comfort. "If Ma-kun wants to help, then we should help, too. Mommy will do whatever she can."

"Mom..."

The perfect mother, one who understood how her son felt, and gave him a gentle push forward...except... "I'd love your help, just make sure you don't try to take over." "R-right. I understand." Parental self-awareness played a vital role in reducing the suffering of children, so he was forced to press that point.

Mamako accepted his admonishment and turned toward Wise. "Given all that, Wise, I'd appreciate it if you could cooperate with Ma-kun here. What do you say?"

"Cooperate, huh? I'm not sure why I should have to cooperate with the urges of Masato's libido..." She stared at him pointedly.

"Take that accusation out of your eyes! My libido is unrelated! Regardless of how this started, right now I'm genuinely just concerned for Medhi!"

"Genuine concern... Riiiight."

Wise took a long look at Masato, mulling it over. And then sighed, as if she had grave concerns.

"All right, all right. I'm a Sage; it's, like, my job to get run ragged by the dumb, pervy, pointlessly hot-blooded hero."

"But our party's hero is an intelligent, reliable, handsome gentleman."

"So *you* say. *Sigh*... But, well, that same busybody bullcrap helped me patch things over with my mom, so...can't really sit this one out, can I?"

"Thanks, Wise. How about you, Porta…? Oh my!"

When Mamako turned toward Porta…

"S-surrrrre… I'll…be glaaaaaaaad…to heeeeeeelp…"

Porta was bright red, her eyes spinning. Her whole body was swaying. Yet somehow the bag stayed on her head. Good job! Though maybe her impeccable balance shouldn't have been their first concern.

"Hey, Porta! You okay there?"

"My goodness! Porta, sweetie, you've been in the bath too long!"

"Crap, that's not good! We'd better get her out!"

Mamako and Wise stood up and quickly moved to tend to Porta.

Two bare behinds moved swiftly through the water…though now may not be the best time to look.

Mamako picked Porta up, and she and Wise left the bath.

"Porta needs to rest! The three of us are leaving the bath first!"

"You stay here awhile! We need to get dressed in the changing room, so you sit right there and count to twenty million before you dare come out! And stop looking this way!"

"R-right… Yes, ma'am…"

Masato averted his eyes, letting the three ladies go.

That meant…

"…I escaped punishment this time, too?"

It wasn't like he'd been looking forward to it. They'd bathed together, he'd seen them naked, and nothing had happened to him. "Guess I should say…thank you?" Masato murmured.

"One…two…three…four. Times five million…is twenty million…"

Masato waited to get out until he'd counted all the way to twenty million. He may have skipped a few numbers along the way, though.

He may not have bothered counting properly, but he'd made extra sure the three of them had definitely left the changing room. He was in the clear. Absolutely clear. Only then did Masato try to open the changing room door.

Just as he did, there was a noise on the other side. Someone had just come in.

This inn only had the one bath. And right now, it was the women's bathing time. Which meant...

...*Uh-oh. This is bad news.*

Beyond bad news. If he ran smack into them, he'd be labeled a creeper for life.

At least he'd better get in there before they started undressing... No, wait, Masato himself was naked.

He was doomed.

I...I-I-I'd better hide!

Masato quickly put the bathtub cover against the wall and hid behind it... If he was found hiding here, he would definitely be mistaken for a Peeping Tom. But what choice did he have?

The door opened, and someone came in. Masato kept his breathing shallow, his eyes tightly shut, promising he wouldn't look...

But the muscles in his eyelids were feeble, and his eyes opened of their own accord, and since they'd opened anyway, he stole a glance—just a glance!—toward the noise.

There, he saw a girl with long hair, large breasts, a thin waist, long legs... The shape of her figure was so beautiful...

Oh... Medhi?!

It was definitely her! That was Medhi! She was right here, naked!

Medhi undid the towel covering her...

...and then flung it as hard as she could at the surface of the water. *Splash!*

Medhi pulled the wet towel out of the water, then flung it down again. *Sploosh!* Then she did it again. Relentlessly, like it had killed her father, over and over and over.

Spitting poison.

"Ughhh... Shit... Self-training before dinner, self-training after dinner... That toxic bitch is driving me crazy... Why won't she just die already?!"

Foul word after foul word came flying out of Medhi's mouth.

Part of him knew how much stress Medhi was under and thought it was only natural she'd end up like this, but...

But watching a beautiful naked girl throw a towel with perfect pitch form was, in all kinds of ways, not something he should be seeing.

"...*Sigh.*"

Without thinking, Masato let out a rather loud sigh. Even though he was supposed to be hiding.

And naturally, she heard him.

"Huh... I-is somebody there?!"

"Oh, crap!" he blurted, sealing his own death warrant. No getting out of this now.

Masato went down on all fours, staring firmly at the floor, and came crawling out.

"Oh... M-Masato?! Why are you here?!"

"Um... Well... Long story short, we've been staying at this inn the whole time, and while I was in the bath, it switched to women's hours, and when I tried to leave, you came in and...here we are."

"Th-that doesn't... We only just started staying here tonight, so... But... Um..."

"I didn't look! I didn't see anything! Totally not looking!" His forehead hit the ground.

"Oh, yes, well, not right now, but...like, a minute ago you were, so..."

"Erp..."

When Medhi's stress-fueled dark power was gushing out of her, he'd heard and seen, so...what should he say?

While he was debating it...

"Medhi? What's all the fuss?"

Medhimama entered the bath. Her alluringly mature body was totally exposed—she might not be quite as young-looking as Mamako, but she was definitely in great shape.

When she saw Masato there, she smiled broadly, the veins on her entire face bulging out. That was far beyond mere anger.

"Oh, Masato. Fancy meeting you here." *Throb, throb, throb, throb.*

"Um... I literally just finished explaining the situation to Medhi here, so I'll let her fill you in. You, uh...go ahead and enjoy your bath."

"You don't say? You certainly don't lack for nerve. Nonetheless, your scummy behavior deserves a fitting punishment, and I shall deliver it personally."

In Medhimama's hand was a different staff from the one she'd broken before. This one had a gem the color of darkness itself. She chanted a spell.

"Spara la magia per mirare! Purificare!"

A magic circle appeared at Masato's feet, and cold light poured out of it.

...Oh, right... Of course...

Enveloped in a light that purified evil thoughts, Masato realized something.

Being blown away in one way or another after any accidental pervert situation was not a matter of a simple violence. It was a punishment.

And after receiving that punishment, many men expressed words of gratitude.

But that gratitude was not directed at the punishment itself. They were grateful to receive a just punishment that alleviated the guilt they felt.

So...

"Thank...you...," Masato said, his heart clear as his body and mind vanished...or so he thought.

...Huh? What is this?

Masato should have been evaporated, but he was still standing in the bath. Not in a coffin but floating above a coffin like a ghost.

Because of the nightly death spells Wise had cast on him since first entering the game, his accumulative death count had reached a high-enough level that Masato's death form had evolved to Ghost.
Congratulations!

My movement is limited... The difference from the standard coffin state is that I can still see around me...

Meanwhile, it didn't seem like anyone else could see Masato in Ghost form.

Medhimama had clearly not noticed what was happening with Masato at all and was standing there naked as the day she was born. He didn't even have to peek. He could stare all he liked. This form certainly had its benefits... Wait, he wasn't looking! He wasn't!

Medhimama looked down at her staff, mildly surprised.

"Oh my. He really was vaporized... That was more powerful than I expected. I wonder if this means my true power has been unleashed... I have no idea who sent this to me, but this Aperto staff is quite powerful. Ohhh-ho-ho-ho!"

"Um, Mother... We really should bring Masato back to life soon..."

"We can do that later. First, Medhi, come here. I'm going to use this release power to really draw out your appeal."

"Huh? ...Wh-what would that accomplish, exactly...?"

"Isn't it obvious? You're going to snare that Masato."

"Snare...him?"

"Yes. Charm him, bewitch him. Your appeal will be so powerful that simply walking by him will make him fall in love with you. And then I'll arrange for the two of you to face off directly...but his love for you will prevent him from doing anything and ensure your victory. Well? Great plan, or greatest plan?"

"Th-that's...something only a coward would..."

"It's perfect! I said it was, so we're doing it! You shut up and do as I say! I grant you the power of this staff!"

Medhimama held Aperto over Medhi's head. Light from the dark gem in the staff poured over Medhi.

"You must win at all costs. You will win. You will be number one. And I will take the utmost pleasure in it. Ohhh-ho-ho-ho!"

Drunk on her own pleasure, Medhimama smiled dreamily.

Her daughter stared at her, utterly baffled.

"...You'll take pleasure in it?" Medhi whispered, visibly upset. "That's all this is for?"

That sure made it clear who really benefited from this.

I agree! That's a dead giveaway.

Floating nearby, Masato was as aghast as Medhi.

Total scores:

Masato: 70 SP. Wise: 45 SP. Porta: 70 SP.

The shop the party had run was a great success. As a reward for that fervor, all of them had received twenty points. And Wise had received a beauty contest consolation prize of five points.

Which was great and all, but perhaps none of that mattered anymore.

The darkness inside the girl was growing stronger and beginning to affect things around her.

Report Card

Student: Porta

Teacher: Mamako Oosuki (Filling in)

Academic Performance

Interested/Focused: Pays Attention, Actively Participates	✓
Speaking/Listening: Articulates Thoughts, Understands Those of Others	✓
Knowledge/Comprehension: Demonstrates These with Regards to Classroom Content	✓
Skills/Expression: Uses Imagination, Expresses Concepts with Their Own Sensibility	✓

Overall Academic Impressions

Tried very hard at everything.

It's so lovely to see her doing her best!

She made all the dishes and aprons we used for the festival stall.

She's so reliable for someone her age.

Such a good girl!

Notes from Parent or Guardian

I'm writing this in place of Porta's mother.

Come to think of it, she doesn't really talk about her mother much. I wonder what she's like...?

I'm sure we'll meet someday, and I look forward to telling her all about what her daughter's done.

Gioco Accademia

Chapter 5 If I Don't Tell Her, She'll Never Get It, but If I Do, She'll Probably Hit Me. Families Are Tough.

The fourth day.

The students gathered beneath a clear blue sky.

"Ahem," Mr. Burly announced. "As I mentioned briefly yesterday, today we have a special school event... A surprise field trip! Let's all have fun with it!"

"Yaaay! A surprise field trip! Woo-hoo!"

"A surprise field trip! I can't wait!"

Apparently, there was a field trip today. Always one of school's greatest pleasures. Wise, Porta, and the other students all cheered.

It was only natural for them to be excited. Not only was the trip itself worth looking forward to, but also they were going to be traveling in style aboard an actual airship.

An airship was, of course, a ship that could fly. As the students clambered aboard the vehicle of their dreams, moored in the school field, they were already far too excited to listen to Mr. Burly, running wild all over the deck.

But there was one student not joining in the fuss. Masato.

"A field trip on an airship... That should be worth looking forward to, but... *Sigh...*"

Masato stayed away from the crowd, leaning against the railing, sighing to himself. He just couldn't convince himself to enjoy this.

And the reason for that was Medhi. His concerns about her were weighing him down.

Then he heard a voice.

"Ma-kun! Have fun! And be careful!"

He looked down and saw Mamako waving him off. Shiraaase was next to her, and Medhimama a short distance away.

Only students were going on this trip. No guardians along. As it should be.

Mamako was calling his name happily, oblivious to his mood, which rubbed Masato the wrong way. He waved a hand back and paid her no further attention.

But then...

"Maasatooo!"

Medhi came running over to him excitedly and latched on to his arm. "Eep?!" Masato yelped, all too conscious of the glorious sensation squeezing against him. Pillowy! His arm shrieked with joy.

He would have loved to enjoy this unreservedly, but he just couldn't. He knew better.

Medhi was acting on Medhimama's instructions and aggressively trying to steal his heart.

"A field trip, Masato! Let's enjoy this together! Just you and me! Let's take this opportunity to get closer!"

"Uh, yeah, sure..."

Medhi pressed up against him, purring in his ear. Sultry expressions, an alluring voice, even her body, using all her feminine wiles to hook him.

Just a hint of desperation.

Everything I was worried about is coming true... How should I handle this?

Unsure of how to respond, Masato just looked confused.

"Hey, Hero Masato! Could you come over here a minute?" Mr. Burly called. Good excuse to get some distance.

"They're calling my name! See you later!" "Um, oh, Masato...!" Masato wriggled out of Medhi's arms and beat an emergency retreat to Mr. Burly's side.

"Sorry for the wait. What's up? Also, thanks."

"That's an odd choice of words, but I suppose you mean I was right to call on you. I got a sense the Cleric Medhi wasn't behaving like herself."

"You're totally right. And the cause is, of course, Medhimama."

"That woman… She is a doozy."

"I agree. She's definitely driving Medhi off the deep end. I don't think we can let it go on like this."

"Hmm, I see." Mr. Burly nodded. "So the hero rises to save families from their problems."

He gave Masato a hearty slap on the back.

"Very well! I will support your heroic fight from the shadows."

"From the shadows? Meaning…?"

"I will do what I can to increase the opportunities for you to spend time with the young Cleric! At least allow me that much. Starting with…"

Rather than finish his sentence, he clapped Masato on the back again and walked away. Masato's back hurt a lot now. There was probably a hand-shaped mark on it.

But it had definitely put some wind in his sails.

"…Guess that was his way of encouraging me. Not that I needed any encouragement…"

Masato looked over the rail at Medhimama, who was glaring fiercely up at them. He looked at Medhi, who was waving, a stiff sort of smile on her face. And then he looked at the sky, so open and free of all worldly concerns.

And he vowed to do something about it all.

Our parents aren't with us on this trip. I've got to take advantage of that!

Forget all their troubles, throw themselves into the event, have as much fun as possible, relieve all that stress. Refresh body and soul. That was what mattered. Only once that was accomplished could he take the next step.

She needed to blow off some steam so she could truly be free.

He knew just what to do. Masato ran back over to Medhi.

"Medhi, thanks for waiting! Let's have a great time on this trip, okay? Let's have so much fun we forget about everything else!"

"Y-yes! That's exactly what I want to do! If I'm with you, Masato, I'm sure I'll have a great time. This is gonna be the best!"

"Yeah! I love it when you talk like this!" *Poke, poke.*

Maybe he got a bit carried away. He found himself poking her in the cheek.

"Eep! Masato, that tickles! Ah-ha-ha!" Medhi laughed happily, enjoying herself. That was good.

If he could keep her this happy and having this much fun, surely all her troubles would be washed away.

The airship took off and flew away, laughter trailing in its wake.

Shiraaase watched it go, then turned to Mamako and Medhimama.

"Well, we've seen the children off safely, so I think it's high time for a little mom conference. What do you say?"

"Oh! Why, yes, that sounds delightful."

A mom conference—a meeting designed to allow mothers to talk freely about their children. A horrible event that leaves all children cowering in fear. Mamako jumped on Shiraaase's suggestion, ready to talk about Masato all night.

Meanwhile, Medhimama seemed far less enthused.

"Not exactly my idea of a good time...but, well... If I consider it a good opportunity to gain information that will ensure my victory, perhaps it wouldn't be the worst idea. That said, it would be extremely awkward if it was just Mamako and me, so I must insist you join us, Shiraaase. What do you say?"

"I'd be honored. Mamako, would you mind if I join you?"

"No, not at all. You're always welcome!"

And with that, the mom conference was confirmed.

Medhimama was running the show. Always the first to take charge.

"Then let's go to the terrace of a café I like. It's a lovely shop only operating for a limited time. You'll need to be in contact with me so I can transport us all there."

"Very well."

"Pardon me."

Shiraaase and Mamako put their hands on Medhimama's shoulders. Medhimama raised her staff…

Mamako's eyes fixed on it.

Oh, how strange… Something feels…off about that…

The Aperto staff, especially the gem of darkness embedded in the tip of it, gave Mamako a vague feeling of anxiety.

The airship flew at a relaxed pace away from the school, arriving at its first destination nearly an hour later. It settled into the landing area as if it owned the place.

The gangways were soon lowered, and the students ran down, having the time of their lives…well, most of them.

"…*Sigh*… I'm so worn-out…"

There was one student dragging himself down the ramp, clutching the railing tight. Masato. Already totally exhausted.

Porta was helping him stay upright, and even she was shaking her head. Wise, behind them, looked outright disgusted.

"Ah-ha-ha," Porta giggled. "You may have gotten a bit too excited."

"Burning up all your energy mid-trip, then collapsing the second we get here? I know the type. We've got a word for those types of people. Idiots."

Wise spoke the truth. "I…can't even argue with that…" Masato admitted.

Then Medhi came running down the ramp behind them.

"Look, look, Masato! We're finally here! Isn't it exciting? Come on, or I'll leave you behind! Come on, come on! Chase meee! Ah-ha-ha-ha!"

As Medhi passed Masato, she tapped him on the shoulder. Then she ran off ahead.

"Ohh… What a sweet scent. A delight to the nose! …Man, Medhi was doing everything I was… She sure has endurance…"

Medhi had been extremely excited the whole time. Her childlike, innocent smile was a wonder to behold.

He couldn't stumble now. Masato summoned all his energy, ready to run off after Medhi.

"First, form a line!" Mr. Burly said. Talk about poor timing. "If you can't line up properly, you get to stay on the airship!"

The crowd of students quickly formed a line, listening to Mr. Burly's speech.

"Let me explain why we're here. First, as training for the full group, all of you are going to be visiting a nearby shrine. Which shrine? Well, take a look at the hill to my right."

Mr. Burly pointed at a midsize green hill. A road wound up the side, and near the top of the hill was a shrine made of stone pillars.

Not a ruin. Clearly a newly made shrine.

"That's where you'll be going. Even from here you can tell how beautiful it is, right? If you've got any questions, ask away. I have lots of information!"

Masato raised his hand.

"Then can I ask what makes this shrine so amazing that we need to take a mandatory field trip to it?"

"Hmm, good question. Truth is...at the moment, that shrine has not been given any historical background. I'm sure some writer in operations is desperately working on it right now."

"Huh? What the...?"

"Listen. I'm not done yet. Um, that shrine will appear as an important ruin in an event they're planning on implementing later on. War and disaster will destroy it, they'll apply the effects of time, and place it in an appropriate field."

"Just like some sort of game... Oh, right, that's exactly what this is."

"So this is the only time you'll be able to see it newly built, in perfect condition. A highly valuable opportunity."

For example. If you could see a Greek shrine at the time it was built, wouldn't you want to? It'd be worth a look, at least. Same principle.

"Right, one warning before we set off. There's a powerful monster on the road to the shrine. One so strong all of us could fight it at once without us having any chance of beating it. It's an insanely strong enemy."

"Um... Then how are we going to get there?"

"Normally, it would be impossible! However! For the sake of this field trip, there's a special field effect applied that strengthens all players! With that blessing, you should be able to make swift work of an enemy you could normally never defeat, receive a massive quantity of high-value gems, and if you're lucky, some rare materials. Doesn't that sound like fun?"

Before Mr. Burly could even finish...

"Masato, let's go!" Medhi said, grabbing his arm and pulling him away. "I've always wanted to come here! I'll lead the way! Come on!"

"O-okay...?"

She was holding his arm awfully tight, and he felt a plush sensation enveloping it... His arm was happy again. Unable to resist, Masato let himself be pulled along with Medhi's whim.

But if they did that, of course the teacher was going to be furious.

"H-hey!" Mr. Burly yelled. "This is a group exercise! You can't just... Mm?"

All the students were gone. The entire class was following Masato and Medhi, making a beeline toward the shrine.

Mr. Burly was standing all alone in their wake.

"...Ahem! Well, as long as you enjoy yourselves! Bwa-ha-ha!" Mr. Burly said with a generous guffaw. "But it sure would have been nice if one of you had asked me along... *Sniff...*" Tears started running down his cheeks.

Medhi had started a stampede, and all the other students were in a headlong dash behind her. Like she'd fired the pistol to start a race up the broad marble road to the shrine.

Masato and Medhi were in the lead. It was hard to run with her clinging to his arm, so they'd switched to holding hands, maintaining their position.

"Come on, Masato! Let's go! Go, go, go!"

"Yeah! Let's do this, Medhi! Go, go, go, go, go!"

Masato ran with all his might, trying to match her level of enthusiasm. Watching over her, hoping that this would all help free her from her worries.

Wise and Porta were hot on their heels.

"*Hahh...hahh...* Hey, wait up! You're...going too fast..."

"Masato! Let us come with you! I want to be with you!"

"Yeah! C'mon! This way, Porta! ...Wise, you should maybe lie down somewhere."

"Like! I! Said! You really need to knock it off with this hot-and-cold routine!"

"And like *I* said, you brought it on yourself... Uh, whaaa?!"

Mid-bicker, Masato saw something unbelievable.

Wise was running along behind him, panting heavily, and right behind her...was a giant carnivorous dinosaur head.

It had popped its head out of a forest by the side of the shrine road and appeared to be targeting Wise. Uh-oh. Wise was about to be swallowed whole.

"Yo, Wise! Behind you! Look! Look behind you!"

"Huh? Yeah, right! Like I'm gonna fall for that one!"

"No, seriously! ...Argh!"

He considered just letting it happen, but...she was technically his friend, so Masato pulled Firmamento and turned to help.

This was a ground foe. Not a great fit for a sword that specialized in flying enemies. He wasn't sure he could win, but he at least had to get a hit in...

Then...

"I'll support you! ...*Spara la magia per mirare... Salire!*"

Medhi's spell activated. A support spell that buffed the power of any attacks. This effect was amplified by the field effect.

Masato's ATK was increased with the force of a supernova.

"Whoaaaaaaaa! I can feel power welling up within meeeee! I can do this! I'm doing this! ...Wise! Duck! Rahhhhh!"

"Huh?! What the?!"

Masato swung his sword horizontally. Wise froze stiff, and it barely missed her head, hitting the hungry dinosaur in the nose.

Splat. Its face split in two. Astonishingly sharp.

Masato defeated the dinosaur!

"Huh? ...Huhhhhh?! What the?! What did I even do?!"

Masato himself was more shocked by this than anyone, but he had, indeed, one-shot it.

Its face yawning open, the dinosaur collapsed, replaced by a shower of precious gems. A whole mountain of dice-like objects.

"Th-th-that's a lot!" Porta yelped and hastily scrambled to collect them.

After the results screen, a series of level-up windows appeared.

Congratulations! Congratulations! Congratulations!

Masato wept manly tears.

"This is the moment I've always dreamed of! I'm getting emotional!"

Tears gushed forth. A hot flood of tears streamed down his cheeks. Yes. This was what Masato had always wanted. A true power trip.

"Masato, you're amazing! That was so cool!"

"Huh? Whoa!"

Medhi jumped on his back, pressing up against him. He could feel everything! His back screamed with joy.

But a mere second later, a hand reached out from the side, grabbed a handful of his shirt, and pulled him away, forcibly separating Masato and Medhi.

The culprit was none other than Wise. She looked pissed.

"Wh-what?"

"Nothing... I mean, I'd love to slap you, but you did just save me, so I'll overlook it this time."

"Well... Thanks, I guess?"

He wasn't sure if gratitude was the right response, but the way Wise was glaring at him was a little different from her usual thing, and that made him cautious.

She glared at him a while longer, then sighed. "Whatever," she said, apparently getting over it. She turned to Medhi. "Hey, Medhi, thanks for helping our stupid hero out. I guess you saved me, too. So thanks. I mean it."

"Oh, sure. You're welcome. I'm always glad to help."

"Mm, thanks… So let's move along. I'm coming, too."

Wise took the lead, walking ahead and waving for them to follow her.

But Medhi stopped her.

"Oh, Wise. Could you wait a second? I'd like to cast a support skill on you as well. If your magic attack is buffed, I'm sure you'll be able to fight in style, too."

"Oh, that sounds good. I'm in the mood for showing off a little. Hit me!"

"Okay. Then… Conforto Staff! Unleash your power!"

Medhi raised her staff, and the hidden function inside activated. As a result…

Wise fell asleep. "…*Zzz…zzzz…*" She just face-planted right where she was and was snoring in seconds.

Medhi smiled as if she'd accomplished something important.

"Good, that's settled."

"Uh, no it's not! Wait, Medhi! What are you doing?!"

"Oh, sorry. I meant to buff Wise's magic attack, but instead I seem to have activated a sleep effect. Whatever effect gets activated is totally random, so I can't control it. It can't be helped."

"Yeah, it can!! I mean, for starters, you could just cast the spell normally instead of using the staff…"

"Oh, good point! You're right, Masato. How careless of me. I just thought how nice it would be to spend time alone with you, and then…"

"Uh…"

She wanted to be alone with him. That was her motivation?

A girl as beautiful as Medhi saying something like that was enough to make any guy go…

"W-well, I guess there is nothing we can do! Ah-ha-ha-ha!"

It was important to jump on these things. Also, the only victim here was Wise, which made it allowable.

Medhi pulled his hand forcibly.

"Come on, Masato! The two of us should be the first to reach the shrine! Let's go!"

"Right, I'm in! Oh, wait... We can't just leave Porta..."

Porta was sitting by the mountain of gems, focused entirely on collecting them. Both hands furiously moving, stuffing them into her bag.

It was adorable, like a bunny digging a hole.

"Oh, Masato!" she said, glancing their way. "I'm not done gathering gems yet! I'd like to come, but this is my role! You go on ahead!"

Cool.

"Porta's such a lovely, dedicated girl... And she really knows how to take a hint! Such a helpful girl! Let's go, Masato! Yeah!"

"Y-yeah..."

The phrasing "take a hint" made all this seem uncomfortably calculated, but oh well.

Medhi's grip on his hand tightened, and she dragged Masato after her, allowing no argument.

And so Masato and Medhi reached the shrine. Well ahead of the rest of their class.

The shrine at the hilltop was magnificent, overwhelmingly so. Elaborately carved Corinthian columns in rows all around, so impressive that even someone with no interest in architecture at all would be awed...

Not that Masato was given time to be impressed.

"What a nice shrine! Shrines are places that house a god. What sort of god comes to your mind, Masato? I'm thinking a goddess of destiny... Yes, our destiny. The two of us visiting, the hand of fate guiding us. We were destined to be together, you know? ...Eh-heh-heh! Maybe I'm getting carried away."

"Uh, yeah... Kinda..."

"Oh, look! There's a sign! There's a limited-time shrine café open now! Let's go in! ...Oh, but...if we share some tea together, everyone will think we're a couple... Oh my, what am I saying? Eep, how embarrassing!"

"Um, well, yeah... I mean..."

Everything Medhi said to him felt specifically designed to capture his heart. She seemed to be really going for the whole "snare Masato" plan.

He'd hoped getting all worked up with her would make her forget all her troubles, but Medhimama's fetters were clearly too tight to shake off. This was frustrating.

If she genuinely just liked me, I'd be thrilled, but...

Unfortunately, that did not seem to be the case.

It was time to make her stop. To free her, he had to make things clear.

Regretting the need to part, he quietly removed his arm from its luxury bed in the valley between her breasts, moved around in front of Medhi, and looked her in the eye.

"Medhi, we need to talk. The truth is, I'm onto you."

"Huh? O-onto...?"

"I know this is just a strategy Medhimama ordered you to use." He spoke slowly, staring into her eyes the whole time. "You want to make me fall in love with you so you can gain an advantage over me. It's a dumb plan. She'd punished me, so I died, but I could still hear everything...so you don't need to try. You don't need to force yourself to act this way. Okay?"

Medhi received his message loud and clear and hung her head. She suddenly seemed really depressed.

"O-oh... You know all about it, huh...?"

"Yeah. Sorry to have eavesdropped, but..."

"No, don't worry about that. I'm the one being rude here. You've got no interest, but here I am forcing myself on you...embarrassing myself, like a total idiot... Ugh... What am I even doing...?"

"...Medhi?"

"This is all my mother's fault. She gives me all these crazy orders, uses that weird staff's power… Yes, I blame that staff… I didn't really want to do this, but here I am doing it… She said some nonsense about granting me 'release power,' whatever *that* means. That's why I'm acting like this! Argghh, that toxic bitch!"

"Stop! Stop! You're releasing all that dark power again! Let's just calm down first, okay?"

She was freaking Masato out a little.

Then…

"Medhi! What are you screaming about? For shame!"

A harsh snarl echoed around them. Masato had heard more than enough of that voice to recognize it instantly. It was Medhimama.

Dressed head to toe in golden robes that could certainly be described as divine, she was walking slowly out from the shadow of the shrine's pillars. Mamako and Shiraaase were trailing after her, looking concerned.

"Medhimama? And…Mom, Shiraaase…? What's going on?"

"We elected to hold a mom conference, so I brought us to the café here. I've been here a number of times, so a simple transfer spell. That hardly matters."

"N-no, it's pretty important…"

"It isn't. And you can hold your tongue, Masato. I am talking to Medhi."

Medhimama paid Masato no further attention, her eyes fixed firmly on Medhi.

The look in her eyes was so severe, you would never think this was a mother looking at her daughter. Medhi cowered before her.

"Medhi, what did you just say?"

"I…I…"

"I could swear I heard you express dissatisfaction toward me. I must have been hearing things. You're a good girl who always does exactly what I say. Right?"

"Y-yes… I…do whatever you say, Mother. You know what's best for me. You work so hard for me. I believe…you do."

Medhi's hands were balled up tight, like she was desperately trying to contain an explosion. She'd said similar things before, and she said them again, as if trying to convince herself, as if forcing herself to believe them. Her eyes squeezed shut, nodding.

Medhimama saw this and sighed.

"You'll do what I say? Then do it. Right now. What is it you should be doing?"

"I...I'll continue my date with Masato! Excuse me!"

Medhi bowed to Medhimama, grabbed Masato's arm, and broke into a run.

From the side, he caught a glimpse of a desperate smile. Tears streaming from the corners of her eyes despite the smile on her face.

"Masato, let's go! Let's do another loop of the road to the shrine! Go, go!"

"...Yeah, okay."

Masato didn't fight her on it. Her grip on his arm was so strong it hurt. He ran with her down the shrine road.

He was painfully aware of just how strong her shackles were, unable to find a way to save her.

Once the visit to the shrine was over, the students clambered back aboard the airship and soared across the evening sky toward their quarters for the night.

They were scheduled to stay in a tower built on high ground, looming over the entire world.

"This tower was built by man in an attempt to reach the realm of the gods! According to design documentation. It's currently a hotel. It's scheduled to be destroyed in an upcoming event, so you're all lucky to get to stay here before it gets babeled. That word is, of course, a verb derived from the Tower of Babel, and it means 'the fruit of years of labor turned instantly into a pile of rubble.'"

Conjugated, you get *babel, babels, babeled, babeling.*

Mr. Burly continued his lecture, but no one was really listening. The second the ship was moored on the tower roof, and when the ramp lowered, the students started running down it.

But one student trailed behind them, his feet heavy: Masato.

"...Guess we'd better go, too."

"Yes! Let's go! Tonight we'll make our love nest here... Ah-ha-ha, I don't mean that, what am I saying? Oh, I can't believe it!"

Masato and Medhi went down the gangway arm in arm.

Ever since their encounter with Medhimama at the shrine, Medhi had been on a nonstop high-energy rampage. She showed no signs of slacking off on the constant attempt to make herself appealing.

At the same time, her hand gripped his tightly, as if trying to tell him something. It was only getting more insistent.

He knew she needed his help. He knew that, but...

...What am I supposed to do? ...What can I do for her?

He didn't know, and that was frustrating. Agonizing.

Whether they knew how he felt or not...well, probably not...Wise was trailing along behind them, grumbling.

"Get a room."

"...Really?" he said, giving her a grim look.

"Um... Forget I said that. I was just making a knee-jerk joke, but even I can tell you aren't in the mood. You're actually kinda scaring me with how serious you look. I'm sorry."

"You've got nothing to be sorry about. Look, if you can find a way to turn this into a farce, please, be my guest. I'd love nothing more."

"Yeah, I don't see that working out. Even I can take a hint, too. If I'm gonna do something, it's gonna need to be something serious. So...Medhi, can I have a minute?"

"S-sure... What is it?"

Wise stepped around in front of them, facing Medhi.

"You need to cut the crap."

Serious expression, level tones, brutal wording.

"You're all over Masato right now, but that's just because Medhi-mama told you to be. Right?"

"W-well..."

"Yeah, okay. Sure. The hesitation tells me everything. You wanna seduce Masato and get him in your pocket. I figured as much. Ain't no way Masato would ever be this popular otherwise. Ever."

"Hey, you jerk, that's too harsh—"

"Shut up, Masato. I'm talking to Medhi."

Masato swallowed his anger. This really didn't seem like something he wanted to interrupt.

"Tell me, Medhi," Wise began. "Just how far are you willing to go on your mom's orders? Doesn't it piss you off at all? Me, I'd totally hate it. I've got a mind of my own, y'know? Don't you?"

"I—I do have a mind of my own. I swear."

"Then prove it! Say what you really want. We're the only ones here. See? What do *you* want? Tell us," Wise insisted.

Medhi thought for a while, and then she let go of Masato's arm, as if she'd made up her mind.

"I just want to enjoy myself. Like a normal person. Here we are on a field trip. I just want to have fun with my friends. But..."

"But what?"

"But I don't have any friends, so I can't do that," Medhi whispered.

"That's not true," Masato said immediately. He took Medhi's arm back, making sure his arm and elbow didn't bump anything inappropriate, and pulled her closer.

He maybe thought that was a little overkill, and he could feel his face burning, but he kept talking.

"You've got a friend right here. I'm your friend."

"Masato... B-but... You must despise me. I mean..."

"I'll be honest. I hate seeing you do whatever Medhimama says. But that doesn't mean I hate everything about you. If you're able to say what you want and act according to your own free will, then I'm ready to enjoy this trip with you as a friend."

"B-but...it isn't just me. My mother will..."

"That's not a problem. I struggle with my own mom sometimes, too. I've built up some pretty decent resistance to mom problems. And us both having similar worries just brings us closer together."

"Th-then...!"

Medhi practically yelped with joy.

"Then let's add another friend," Wise added. She stepped up next to Medhi, on the opposite side, and took her other arm.

"Wise? ...You'll be my friend, too? Really?"

"It'd be weird for your only friend to be a guy, right? You're definitely gonna need someone around to protect you from Masato's ulterior motives. I've got your back there. And I've got mom-poison resistance in spades. That won't be a problem for me, either."

"Then—then...!"

"Now, Medhi. You gotta say this real loud. Tell us what you wanna do, of your own free will."

Masato shot her his best cool-guy smile.

Medhi looked from him to Wise.

"Ohhh... Ohhhhhhhh...!"

She let out a wordless squeal. She hopped back and forth a few times, arm in arm with both of them. "Dancing with joy, huh?" "Then there's nothing left to say." "But—but!"

Like a small child, Medhi hopped around, shedding tears of joy with a huge smile on her face.

"I want to have loads of fun with my friends! I want to do what *I* want, not what my mother tells me to do! I want us all to have a great time together!"

"Okay, roger that! Let's get this party started! It's a field trip, after all! Forget all your troubles and laugh it up with your friends!"

"That's what it's all about! Let's get going!"

""Yeah!""

Spirits high, the three of them headed toward the tower, arms linked together.

Wait, only three?

"Mm? Where's Porta?

Can't forget her. Porta was vital. Where had the world's greatest treasure gone off to? Masato looked around...

...and found Porta at the edge of the roof, crouching before the railing, staring over the edge.

"Um, Porta? Something wrong?"

"Oh, yes, um... I was looking at the scenery and thought I saw someone down below... Maybe it was..."

"Maybe it was...?"

"Oh, no, never mind. It was too dark to see, so I can't say for sure! Sorry!"

Porta bobbed her head.

Then she stood there fiddling her thumbs, staring at them, clearly envious of their locked arms.

"Um, uh, if I could, too…"

""Don't even bother finishing!""

Masato and Wise both reached out. All arms linked, the four formed a circle.

"Yay! A circle of friends!" "This is gonna make it hard to move, though." "But it's so much fun!" "I'm glad I can have fun with you!" Objectively, this was extremely silly. But that didn't mean it wasn't fun!

And then Mr. Burly called out to them.

"Hey, Hero Masato and party! Head on into the tower already! You're the last ones!"

"Oh, yeah! Sorry! We're coming!"

"Mm. Make sure you do. Oh, Hero Masato…about the room assignments…"

Mr. Burly did not explain further. He simply winked broadly.

Apparently, he was keeping his word on the whole "give Masato and Medhi time together" thing…

They'd been assigned to a room on the top floor of the tower. Fantastic view. The interior was all imposing stonework, giving the room a hard-core fantasy feel.

But it was a room for four. Two beds on either side of the room. Four beds total.

"This is every night for me," Wise said, "so I'm used to it by now, but are you okay with this, Medhi? If you're not down sharing with a boy, we could talk to Mr. Burly and try to get him moved."

"I'm fine with it. I'd rather be with my friends. I think it's great we're all together."

"Okaaay, as a wholesome young man, I think it's my duty to wholesomely share a bed with Porta!"

"Okay! I'll sleep with you!" Porta sparkled. ☆

"Gah! That pure gaze blinds me! I genuinely had no illicit motives, yet it burns the heart all the same!"

In the end, each slept in their own bed. Obviously.

Masato and Medhi on the right, Wise and Porta on the left, each picked a place. "Shall we?" "Of course." "I'm in." "Me too!" "Right then, on three!" All four of them did a dive and landed flat on their beds.

With everyone here, Masato felt safe. In a mood for smiling for no particular reason, he made a proposal.

"We've got time before dinner, so let's decide how we want to use our free time tomorrow. Assuming, of course, we're all spending it together. Anyone have any bright ideas?"

Everyone mulled this over.

"Well," Wise said, "we could start by exploring this tower. I mean, they're gonna knock the place down eventually. Seems a waste not to check it out while we're here."

"Yes! I agree! …Oh, but…it is a very big tower, so I'm scared we'll get lost."

"Hmm… Field trips are supposed to be fun, so wearing ourselves out getting lost in a dungeon…maybe not ideal."

"Yeah, good point…"

It was a good idea, but maybe there was something better. Everyone thought some more.

"I can guide us around the tower," Medhi said. She seemed fairly confident. "I've actually been here before. Mom said she wanted to stay in a room at the top of the world, so we took a pretty good look around."

"This another side effect of her obsession with superiority? Sure sounds like something she'd do. But let's not think about that. If Medhi can be our guide…"

Masato glanced at Wise and Porta, and both nodded. That settled it.

Masato stood up on his bed, looking around the room. Like a hero. Like a leader.

"Your attention, please. Tomorrow, we will embark on an adventure. This will be a true adventure. For children, by children, with only children on it. No parents allowed!"

"The more you say that, the more likely they are to just show up," Wise muttered.

"Whoaaa, Wise! Don't scare me like that!"

"That won't happen, will it?!" Medhi yelped. "We'll be okay, right?!"

They were probably safe, but just in case... "Medhi!" "Yes!" They two of them could cover more ground. They checked outside the room. Clear. Outside the windows. Clear.

No parents? Really no parents? No signs of them. Good. Masato and Medhi each breathed a sigh of relief and sat back down on their beds.

"Ahem, so, tomorrow it'll be just us," Masato said. "It'll be great. We'll have a lot of fun. A great, big, exciting adventure. All of us together. The end!"

A rousing finish. A round of applause.

Next...

"So that covers our plans for free time tomorrow, but there's still time before dinner, so next...I guess we should talk about what to do now."

Masato was enjoying this whole party-leader thing. But when he tried to advance the discussion...

Something soft smacked him in the face. A pillow. Flung right at him.

And the culprit...was Medhi.

"A field trip, in your hotel room, time on our hands, friends to have fun with... That calls for one thing! I've always wanted to try it, but this is the first chance I've had!"

Masato had never seen Medhi's eyes sparkle quite so brightly. It was obvious how excited she was about this.

Who was he to argue? He was fully ready to live up to her

expectations. Masato stole a glance in the other direction and saw Wise and Porta ready with their own pillows.

There was only one thing for him to say.

"Okay! This means war!"

And the pillow fight began. He flung a pillow. "Mmph?!" "Pfft! Serves you... Bwah?!" Someone hit him. "Porta, get ready!" "Mm! I won't lose!" There were pillows flying everywhere.

It was Wise who brought a shift in the stalemate.

"Riiight, then I summon Porta! I equip her with my pillow and attack Masato with an unavoidable Porta attack!"

"Wh-whaat?! An unavoidable Porta attack?!"

"Ha-ha-ha! Go get him, Porta!"

"Okay! Masato, here I go! Hyah!"

Porta tossed a pillow his way. Her thin little arms did not exactly put a lot of force behind the throw, and her aim was way off...but it was an unmissable attack! "Unh!" Masato grunted, diving to one side so the Porta attack would hit him right in the face. *Poof*, direct hit. Yay! Getting hit was pure bliss.

But this was a competition.

"Unh! Two against one is hardly fair! This calls for...Medhi!"

"Yes! I've got your back, Masato!"

Medhi raised her staff and chanted a spell.

"Here I go! ...*Spara la magia per mirare... Salire!*"

"Rahhhhhhhhh! I can feel the power coursing through meeeee!"

Medhi's spell strengthened Masato's attack. **Masato threw a pillow with extra force!** "Take thaaaat!" "Yeeek!" **The pillow hit Wise in the face! She made a strange noise! Hilarious!**

"H-hey, using magic is cheating!"

"Huh? How? It's totally fine... Right, Medhi?"

"Yes. Since the magic spell was not a direct attack, there should be no concerns. This is a pillow fight, and Masato threw a pillow. That is all. Heh-heh-heh."

"Oh yeah? Then I've got a plan of my own... Porta! Let me have that pillow!"

"O-okay! Here!"

Wise took a pillow in each hand, chanting a spell.

"...*Spara la magia per mirare... Bomba!* And! *Bomba!*"

Wise's chain case activated. The two pillows were granted explosive properties.

Two pillow-shaped bombs ready for detonation.

"Whoa, wait! That's cheating! Outright criminal! Terrorism!"

"Huh? How so? They're just pillows. Pillows are always okay... Heh. Heh. Heh... Fly, my pillows! After him!"

"Hey, wait! ...M-Medhi! Maybe some magic defense...?!"

"Good luck, Masato! Yay! **Barrier.**

"Huh?! Medhi, did you just put up a barrier spell around yourself?! While clearly enjoying my inevitable demise?!"

"Don't worry, Ma-kun! Mommy's got your back!"

"Oh, that's a relief! Your two-hit multi-target— Wait... Hey!"

Weird. He felt like he'd heard a voice that had no business being here.

Masato turned his head with an audible creak, checking next to him...and there stood a mom, holding a pillow in each hand, ready for a two-pillow attack. Like she belonged there.

It was Mamako.

"Huh? ...Whaaaaat?! Wh-why are you here?!"

"Well, Medhimama wanted to come see how Medhi was doing, so I tagged along..."

No sooner did Mamako explain than an all-too-familiar screech echoed through the room.

"Medhi! Why are you playing games?! What nonsense is this?"

Already at peak rage, Medhimama walked over to where Medhi stood stunned, grabbed her violently by the collar, and dragged her out of the room. "M-Mother! That hurts...!" "What do I care?" Nothing motherly left about her, just pure severity.

As Medhi was forcibly dragged out of the room, Masato was left spluttering, "...Ah, w-wait! Wait!"

He hurried out into the hall after them.

*   *   *

Medhimama had Medhi pinned to the wall, spitting a torrent of abuse at her.

"Did I tell you to go play games?! I didn't, did I? I told you to make Masato yours, didn't I? Why aren't you doing what I said?!"

"W-well, it was a field trip, so..."

"Who cares about some stupid field trip?! You disobeyed me, and that's the only thing that matters here! Why don't you ever listen to me?!"

"B-because I... Masato and... They're my friends... I wanted to be... They're the first friends I've ever had, so..."

"Shut up! You don't need friends! You need to be number one! That's all! That's the only thing you need! Why can't you understand that? ...Arghhh... You'll need a *real* punishment for this!"

Medhimama raised her staff. This time she was finally going to hit her daughter with it. "Hey!" "Whoa, stop!" "Stop that!" Masato's party came running down the hall to try to stop her, but...

Before they could, a gust of wind... No, a person went flying past them.

Trailing a sweet, gentle fragrance in her wake, the two Holy Swords in hands reached out and caught the staff as it fell.

"I think that's quite enough of that," she said, fixing Medhimama with a stern gaze.

It was Mamako.

She'd coming running with godlike speed, repelled the staff with her swords, and was speaking calmly to Medhimama, who practically frothed with rage.

"Medhimama, if I may have a word."

"You may not! Who do you think you are?! Why do you always stick your nose in other people's business?! You're a plague!"

"I apologize for anything I may have done to upset you, Medhimama. But nonetheless, I will speak my mind... For any mother, it's a delight when your child manages to be number one. I know exactly how that feels. After all, I am a mother, too."

"Yes! Any mother would want their child to be the best! Any mother would do everything in their power to make that happen! I've done nothing wrong!"

"But I don't think that's any excuse to force your children to do things they don't want to do. There's no reason that Medhi should have to suffer like this just for the sake of being number one."

"There is! Medhi has to be number one! After all...!"

"If my daughter is number one, that makes me the number one mother! I need Medhi to be the best child around so that I can be the best mother!"

This declaration echoed down the hall. Not for her daughter, not for anyone else, but just for her own personal glory.

This seemed to catch even Mamako off guard, and she was left at a loss for words. Not able to think of any way to argue. Masato, Wise, and Porta were equally shocked.

But in the silence that followed, Medhi began to whisper.

"...*Sigh*... Enough. Enough."

Resignation on her face, Medhi took a step toward Medhimama, raising her staff.

Abandoning all thoughts and feelings, ready to beat her mother with it.

"Whoa, Medhi! Wait!"

Masato couldn't let that happen. He jumped in her way. Medhi didn't care. She swung the staff anyway.

Masato stuck out his left hand, deploying his shield wall and catching it. "Unh...!" The blow was too strong, and Masato's hand hurt quite a lot.

"Wh-what are you doing?!" Wise said, running to help. "Have you lost your mind, Medhi?!"

"I-I-I'll get a sedative...!" Porta spluttered.

"No, I got this!" Masato said. "Just let me deal with her! I'll talk to Medhi!"

On the surface, Medhi appeared almost frighteningly calm. But the black torrent of emotions churning beneath the surface could not be taken lightly.

"Medhi, don't! Calm down! Think this through!"

"Out of my way. Don't try to stop me."

"I can't let you do this! ...Medhi, I need you to take a breath here! Please! ...You know you can't raise your hand to your mother, right?"

"So what if I do? ...She's stolen my freedom, and now she wants me to throw away my friends... And all so she can be the best mother? ...Anyone who talks like that isn't fit to be a parent!"

"Y-yeah, what she said was pretty inexcusable, but...!"

"Masato, I've been enduring this for years. Everything she's ever done has only hurt me, made me suffer, made me miserable...but I believed it was all done for my benefit. I was only able to endure it all because I trusted she had my best interests at heart. But she betrayed that trust, and now I've had enough. She can't be allowed to get away with this. I've got to make her pay for what she's done!"

"And I get that!"

"How can you?! You don't know what it's like!"

"I do! Of course I do! I've got... I've had... I've suffered plenty under my own mother!"

Sent into a game with mom in tow. Masato had endured all manner of hardship as a result.

He had earned the right to understand. He knew better than anyone.

Masato was speaking from personal experience.

"Listen, Medhi. When things didn't go the way I wanted, I lost it. But every time I threw a tantrum, I regretted it. I felt like I'd done something so pathetic. I hated myself for it every time! You have to get ahold of yourself. Just take a deep breath..."

"Shut up! Shut up, shut up, shut up!" Medhi roared. His words weren't getting through to her. "I don't care what happens! ...Conforto Staff! Unleash your power! Release all of me!"

A spell activated, and she transformed.

A magic mist spewed out of the tip of her staff, covering her body.

The mist enveloping her expanded explosively, forming a massive torso, four legs, a long tail, and scales… The body of a dragon.

A dragon whose bloodshot eyes screamed with rage and pain. The explosive birth of the Medhidragon.

"*SHE WILL PAY! FOR EVERYTHING!!!*" the Medhidragon shrieked.

Her head reared back and burst through the ceiling. Her powerful tail thrashed, reducing the walls to rubble, heedless of the consequences.

"Argh, so much for calming down! She just got worse instead!"

How was he supposed to go up against this? Retreating from the destruction and flying rubble, Masato racked his brain for a solution.

Then, from behind him…

"Medhi! What on earth is that? You're hideous! Is this how hideous a girl who doesn't listen to her mother becomes? I hate it! This is disgusting! I can't believe you would do this to me!"

Medhimama's own anger showed no signs of subsiding, and she was pouring more fuel onto the fire.

"*YOU'RE THE DISGUSTING ONE!*" Medhidragon roared.

Explosions echoed in every direction.

"Geez! What is *wrong* with these two? You can't talk sense into either of them!"

"Ma-kun, we'll have to divide and conquer! Mommy will handle Medhimama, so the rest of you take care of Medhi, okay?"

"R-right! That's what I was about to suggest! Let's do that!"

Masato and Mamako stood back to back between monster mom and monster daughter, pushing off each other, each breaking into a run.

Mamako launched herself at Medhimama.

"Medhimama, let's go!"

"*Tch*, you again! That's it, I'm taking you on!"

Staff and swords clashed, locking together, but Mamako had momentum on her side and pushed Medhimama backward, away from Medhi.

At the same time, Masato sprang into action.

"We're holding Medhi back! Wise! Porta! Gimme a hand!"

"Okaaay! I'm gonna beat every last ounce of sanity back into her! What else are friends for?!"

"I'll help, too! Leave the items to me!"

"Thanks! ...All right, let's do this!"

Masato's party ran toward Medhidragon.

The battle began with a Tacere. "Ahhh?!" Wise, naturally, had her magic sealed immediately, rendering her useless. Masato was forced to fight alone while Porta readied a Rilascio only for Wise's magic to be immediately sealed again.

A short distance from that titanic struggle, Mamako was facing off with Medhimama.

Medhimama was ready to throw down.

"When you think about it, this is the perfect chance! The outcome of this fight will prove which of us is the better mother! ...Aperto staff! Show me your power!"

Medhimama raised her staff. The dark gem embedded in it unleashed the power of full release, bathing the stone hallways in dim light. The walls, floors, and ceiling all began to move.

Released from being mere rock, the stones began swarming together, becoming golems and attacking Mamako. Charging at her, swinging powerful arms...

But...

"I'm sorry. I only want to talk to Medhimama," Mamako said softly. "So I'll just need you to behave, if you don't mind. Please?"

As she spoke, Terra di Madre began to glow.

The golems all nodded. "...Huh?" Fell apart. "What? How? Why?!" And turned back into the original materials, the walls and floors re-forming. The hallway was back to normal.

Medhimama was so shocked her jaw nearly dislocated.

"Wh-whaaaaat? H-how?! What did you just do? Why are the golems I made obeying your orders?!"

"I didn't give them any orders. I just asked them nicely... Although, the difference between the two can be so hard to find... I worried about that a lot, myself."

"What do you mean...?"

"This was back when Ma-kun was still little... I was always fretting that everything I said to my son would be imposing my will upon him... I used to write down what I wanted to say and spend days thinking about the best way to put it."

"What's the point?! They should be doing what you say! Parents should raise their children as they see fit! That's how it works, isn't it?!"

"Well, I do think that's part of it... But there is one mistake you must never make."

"And what would that be?!" Medhimama shouted, ready to go for the throat.

Mamako put her swords away, facing her with a gentle smile.

Then Mamako's body began to glow. And her body began to float just above the ground. Like a god manifesting itself in the world.

The God-Mother Mamako spake unto Medhimama thusly:

"It is the job of the parent to raise the child into an upstanding adult. We are not raising our children for our own benefit. Our words, our feelings, our entire beings must be poured into helping them grow up happy and healthy. Everything is for the child's benefit, and the child's benefit alone."

The light Mamako emitted was not **A Mother's Light**.

She had something she needed to say, as a mother—and when Mamako felt that from the bottom of her heart, she became a focal point for the emotions of mothers the world over, granting her the power to communicate her feelings fully in light and words.

The advanced mom skill, **A Mother's Revelations**.

The motherly light Mamako gave off illuminated her surroundings. That light poured into the staff in Medhimama's hands...and a moment later, there was a crack, and a fissure ran across the dark gem embedded in it.

Medhimama snapped out of her stupor.

"O-obviously! All mothers think... Um... But wait, I just...I spoke as if it was all for me... Wh-why would I say that...?"

"Medhimama, please calm down. You were under the influence of something sinister. Relax."

Mamako settled to the ground in front of the flustered Medhimama, patting her shoulder. Being as nice as possible, steadying her nerves.

"There's nothing wrong with you now," she reassured her. "You know what really matters... No matter how harsh you were with her, your daughter trusted you and followed you. She was most precious to you, most devoted to you, and now you can place her needs first."

"My...my daughter has always come first... Medhi... Oh, Medhi! Where is she? What happened to her?!"

You didn't need to listen very hard to hear a shriek of pain.

"I TRUSTED HEEEEEEEEEEERRRRRRR!"

No matter how monstrous her form, no mother could ever mistake their daughter's voice.

"Medhi! I'm coming! I have so much I need to tell you!"

Medhimama turned and ran.

Mamako stayed behind, smiling gently, watching a mother run to her daughter.

Medhidragon's rampage showed no signs of subsiding. Her tail thrashing, her horns thrusting, she attacked everything in sight. She seemed to be particularly invested in body-slamming every wall around.

Dealing with the shock waves of all this had left Masato and Wise pretty beat-up.

"Hey, Masato. Look back that way! Mamako's doing something pretty insane, even by her standards!"

"Can't let myself be distracted by it! Don't wanna know, either! However many dimensions my mother conquers, I'm better off not knowing! ...Oh, she's locked onto you!"

"...SPARA LA MAGIA PER MIRARE... MASSORBENTE!"

"Huh? Aughhhhh?!"

Medhidragon's spell absorbed MP. All of Wise's MP was drained away.

"Heeeey!! What the hell?!" "Stop yelling and get down!" Masato put up his shield wall, defending Wise, focusing on defense.

"This whole darkness element sure makes her drain spells effective…"

"A dark healer is super annoying! Ugh, this is seriously pissing me off! We gotta do something!"

"If you feel that way, go recover your MP! I'm running low on HP myself! Hurry!"

"I know! …Porta! Can I get an MP Potion?"

"Yes! Here!"

As a Mage, Wise needed a lot of MP. Porta ran in holding a bunch of MP Potion bottles. Wise chugged them all. "Ugh… My stomach didn't like that…" "Here's another! Go ahead!" "O-okay…" Porta had no idea how relentless she was being.

Masato had no time to pay this any attention. Medhidragon was attacking again.

"*AH-HA-HA! NOTHING MATTERS! I DON'T CARE ANY-MORE! AH-HA-HA-HA!*"

"Unh!"

Masato was running out of durability to soak the onslaught. It was physically demanding work.

But emotionally, he was still ready to go. He had a lot of words left to fling at her.

"Medhi! I know all too well how that feels! So please listen to me!"

"*YOU DON'T KNOW! NOBODY KNOWS HOW I FEEL!*"

"Of course I do! I've got a mom, and she makes life miserable for me all the time! Makes me wanna cough up blood sometimes!"

"*NO WAY! MAMAKO IS A GREAT MOM!*"

"How?! Just having a mom along inside a game is a living night-mare! Then she's all wearing sailor uniforms and school swimsuits and winning beauty contests… I'm constantly running into stuff I'd rather wipe from my mind entirely! I'm seriously at my wit's end here!"

When he'd first seen his mother wearing a sailor uniform, the blow had been severe; his hands had clenched so tight, blood spurted out of them. And not just his hands—every blood vessel in his body had been ready to burst.

To a stranger, it might just be a funny story. But to Masato, it was no laughing matter.

The wounds had healed, but the emotional scars still festered inside him.

Still…

"But even so, I'm not throwing a tantrum like a little kid! That won't resolve anything! It'll just open all the wounds!"

"THEN WHAT SHOULD I DO? WHAT ELSE IS THERE?!"

"First, communicate! Use your words, tell her how you feel, what you want! I still haven't managed to get it across, either, but that's where you have to start!"

"WHY TALK WHEN SHE WON'T LISTEN?!"

"If you give up without trying, then everything just gets bottled up inside you! And this is the result! You have to change that, or… Urk?!"

Medhidragon's tail scored a direct hit on him. Her rampage was definitely very childish. No matter what he said, nothing was getting through to her. At this rate, she was going to push him away…

But then Medhimama came running over.

"Masato, stand down!"

It seemed she wanted to face Medhidragon herself.

"No, wait! Medhi's attacks are really strong! I'm a hero and even I'm struggling! You're just a healer…!"

"What does that matter? …If she's being violent, then all the more reason I should bear the brunt of it! I can't let my child hurt someone else's! …Yes, that's right… I must be the one to take this! I'm her one and only mother!"

Medhidragon glared at Medhimama, howling like a mad thing.

"TOO…TOO LATE TO PRETEND LIKE YOU CARE!"

Her tail came swinging in from one side.

Medhimama tried to catch it with the Aperto staff, but Medhidragon had put too much force behind it. "Gah!" Medhimama was flung aside, slamming into a mountain of rubble. The staff fell from her hand.

A direct hit from a blow with fatal force...yet Medhimama got back up.

Staring up at her daughter's new form, she bit her lip, holding it in.

"*Sigh...* Honestly, I don't know how I have the nerve to act like a mom now."

"*I'LL NEVER FORGIVE YOU! NOT EVER!*"

"Medhi...you're really scary right now," Medhimama whispered. "You've been bottling feelings like this up inside you all along, but you trusted me and followed me... You're quite amazing."

Medhimama faced off against Medhidragon once more.

Despite the situation, there was nothing but kindness on her face. Masato blinked.

Oh... For once, Medhimama is actually being a mom.

He couldn't quite put his finger on it, but there was definitely something mom-like going on there. Masato was sure of that.

Maybe this was some sort of skill. That wasn't clear.

But Masato started running. Like he'd suddenly realized what he had to do, he quickly placed himself in front of Medhimama. Soaking the next blow aimed at her.

"Unh! ...Yep, pretty rough."

"Masato! I said stand down! This is my...!"

"I know! You're the only one who can resolve this mess! But we aren't getting anywhere this way! First, we've gotta do something about Medhi!"

"What...what can we do?"

"I got this! I'm a hero who saves the bonds between parents and children! So trust me! ...Wise! You ready?"

The Sage had finished replenishing her MP and called back, "Okay! Ready when you are! I know exactly what you're thinking! ...Porta, you'd better keep your distance!"

"Okay! Good luck!"

When she was sure Porta was on safe ground, Wise started chanting.

"...*Spara la magia per mirare... Bomba Vento!* And! *Bomba Vento!*"

Wise's powerful chain cast wind mage activated, striking Medhidragon's legs. The explosive winds lifted her, leaving her massive body floating in the air.

Flying enemies were tailor-made for our powerful hero. Buffeted by the comfortable back draft, Masato tightened his grip on Firmamento. He raised it high above him, prepared to deliver a crushing blow.

"Even Wise gets it right sometimes! Now it's time to give this naughty child the appropriate punishment... Wait, what?!"

Just as Masato was about to unleash a shock wave...

The Aperto staff rose up off the floor somehow, hovering in front of Medhidragon.

A dim light emerged from the staff, and the rubble the light hit rose up, forming a defensive wall to protect Medhidragon.

"Hey, hey, hey, what the hell? What's going on?! ...Dammit, why would you make the defensive shell thicker?!"

Masato quickly swung the sword, striking the wall of rubble with his shock wave. But the wall was too strong, and he couldn't get through. Medhidragon was now completely out of sight.

And then...

"Then let's see how Mommy's attacks do! Hyah!"

Her voice was immediately followed by countless rock spikes and water bullets. Each AOE attack was monstrously powerful at the best of times, and this time they had only one target—nothing to divide up the damage. The overwhelming force of this onslaught easily cut through the wall.

One rock spike severed the staff, and one water bullet pierced the gem of darkness, shattering it. Instantly, the rubble forming the wall crumbled and fell to the ground.

It was obvious who was responsible for this. Masato glanced back where the attack had originated and saw Mamako smiling at him, a flame-red sword in one hand and a deep blue sword in the other.

"Geez... For all the trouble you cause, you sure know exactly when to step in sometimes. Guess that's part of being a mom, huh?"

Not nearly as put out as he sounded, Masato turned to attack again.

Ready to slice through the horrible emotions shrouding Medhi.

No matter what explosions the heart unleashed, deep down, there was still part of her that just wanted to love the person who mattered most.

"The one you care about most is waiting for you with open arms! Give her a good hug and tell her everything you've ever wanted to say! Hahhhhh!"

Masato swung Firmamento with all his might. The massive shock wave that came out was not the usual one but one with a warm glow.

This shock wave sliced only what it should slice; it struck Medhi-dragon, cutting only the shell of turbulent emotion.

"Good! Just as I planned! ...Oh, Medhi!"

As the sides of the monster fell away, the real Medhi appeared from inside. She fell slowly to the ground, cradled by the wind. Masato...stayed right where he was.

The one who should be there to catch her ran forward. Medhimama.

"Medhi!"

She caught her daughter, holding her tight. Her daughter struggled, trying to free herself, but she wouldn't let go. She held her with all her might.

"I'm sorry," Medhimama said.

Tears ran down her daughter's cheeks.

"D-don't say that... I swore...I swore I wouldn't forgive you! I'm done forgiving you! I always do that, and..."

She kept insisting, but she gradually stopped struggling. In time, she was sobbing quietly in her mother's arms.

"...When I first learned this child was growing inside me, I wondered if I could ever be a good mother," Medhimama slowly began.

Medhi was leaning against her. "What made a mother good? How could I be a good mother? That's all I thought about. I looked it up online, I ran out and bought books...and it was one of those. Maybe you've read it, Mamako. It was a bestseller when both of us would have been with child."

"Oh, do you mean *If You Want to Be a Good Mother, Raise a Good Child*? I remember reading a book with that title."

"Yes, that one. You read it, too...yet you certainly have raised a very different child. I wonder where I went wrong."

Medhimama shook her head ruefully.

"I decided to raise my daughter properly and did everything I could think of. We studied every day. I made sure she balanced book learning with physical activity. And...I considered her mental health to the degree I deemed it necessary."

"I've got a lot of doubts about whether that was actually enough."

"Yes, Masato. You might be right. It wasn't nearly enough. To raise a daughter who always did what I said, I micromanaged her heart, overriding her free will. And as a result, I placed an enormous burden on her. It's all my fault."

"Mother..."

"Apologizing for it now doesn't fix what I've done, but at least let me say it. I really am sorry."

There were tears in her eyes. She put her arms around Medhi, pulling her close.

"I knew you were stressed-out. I saw you kicking the wall, swearing under your breath... I knew you were in a bad state. I knew it was all my fault. That's why I wanted to join this game. I thought we could somehow fix the problems between us here. But then I forgot all that somehow...and finally said what I said. I don't know why I... I'm an awful person."

"No, hold on. It's too soon to say that," Masato said, interrupting her. He looked behind him. "Yo, Wise, Porta? What you got?"

"Mm... Yeah... I've got a nasty hunch about it, personally. Reeks kinda like when my mom was being a total idiot... Hmm, I dunno how to describe it... How about you, Porta?"

"I appraised it but was unable to determine the materials or effects! I've never encountered any equipment like this before!"

They were both investigating the Aperto staff. Wise was scowling at it with deep suspicion, and even with her skills, Porta had been unable to get any useful information.

Unknown, huh? What does that mean?

He would much rather have found some conclusive evidence.

But for now, he could make good use of that inconclusive evidence.

"...Medhimama, that staff seems to have some sort of effect that releases darker impulses. When you powered her up with it, Medhi turned into that dragon."

"Huh? Oh, well, yes... That does seem to be..."

"So it seems possible that you were also under the influence of it. Your desire to be a good mother was strengthened and twisted. When you spoke those words, it wasn't what you really meant. You were just at the mercy of some weird power. Before then, you weren't acting for yourself. You really were acting for Medhi's benefit. I think that's safe to say, right?"

"I'm sure of it. I didn't put my daughter through all this just so that I could be the best mother. I only wanted to raise Medhi right... But as for the results..."

"No, Mother. I'm glad you said that."

She'd been strict, but it was all for Medhi. Medhi had been right to have faith in her mother. She hadn't been betrayed. The love between them was real.

Medhi hugged her mother back. And this time, she spoke from the heart.

"You've been strict because you thought it was best for me. And I'm really glad you feel that way. But...I would really like it if you spent as much time considering *my* feelings and *my* needs. Can you promise me that?"

"I promise," Medhimama said. "I'm going to change. I want to be the kind of mother who always puts your needs first. I hope you'll still be my daughter."

"Yes, Mother. I will always be your daughter."

They embraced again, strengthening the bonds between them.

Masato's party watched, smiling.

"Well, Medhi's rampage is over, the air between them is cleared up, everyone's said their piece, and now we just have to see how successful Medhimama is at changing. All's well that ends well."

"Yes. Everyone!"

"Well done?"

"Yes! Well done!"

Hands were raised, clapped, and high-fived. Strategy complete.

And then two late arrivals entered.

"Oh," Mr. Burly said. "Looks like everyone's having fun!"

"It seems everything's been taken care of. Excellent news," Shiraaase said.

"Mm? What's up?"

"What's up? We heard the sounds of a furious battle and came to see what was happening! I planned to step in and help, if necessary, but it seems I was too late!"

"In my case, I deliberately arrived late, keeping my own personal safety paramount, but it seems this was the perfect timing."

"You seem to be your usual self, Shiraaase."

"Either way, all problems with the Cleric Medhi appear to be resolved! Enjoy what's left of the field…"

"You'll be able to take the exam the day after tomorrow with clear hearts and minds. Heh-heh-heh."

"…What?"

Shiraaase had muttered something under her breath that Masato hoped he'd misheard.

But school was school, after all.

Epilogue

The two halves of the Aperto staff lay on the desk in the headmaster's office.

Shiraaase was staring calmly down at it. She let out an annoyed sigh.

"Honestly, for something like this to show up... It's rather vexing."

A staff that released the darker impulses of the heart.

No equipment like this had been designed for the game. Officially.

Shiraaase had double-checked with Operations just to be sure. The facts were clear. What lay in front of her were the remains of a weapon that should never have existed.

But even if she hadn't checked, no data made for a game should ever be able to directly affect the human heart.

Yet, this staff was real.

"We must investigate how it came to exist and what purpose it was intended to serve...but we know absolutely nothing about it, so the Aperto staff itself will likely be a dead end."

So the investigation would have to focus on the purpose.

In that department, at least, they had some hints.

"The power to release their hearts, given to a test player... What can that mean...?"

This game invited parents and children with all kinds of relationship problems to serve as test players. One or both were inevitably harboring some sort of issue.

And unleashing that caused ruptures that went far beyond a mere prank.

Rather than improve their relationship by adventuring together, this would exacerbate the problem...

At worst, it would cause a permanent rift between them.

"And if that happens, this game is a failure. It will end before the official release ever happens. Hmm… Maybe their goal is to end the service… There were certainly any number of parties critical of the game's creation."

Mulling this over, Shiraaase let her gaze drift.

A nearby clock caught her eye. The hour was later than she'd expected.

"Oh dear. I'll be late for the party. She was nice enough to invite me! I simply must show up in time to enjoy Mamako's cooking."

And with that, Shiraaase left the headmaster's office.

Leaving her problems lying on the desk.

"I don't know who you are, but if you want a fight, you've got one… The hero family members are awakening to their true power, and they'll be ready for you. Heh-heh-heh."

Shiraaase smiled, her confidence lying entirely in someone else, someone she had not even consulted about this. Typical.

The seventh day of school. The final day of the special accelerated course.

With the entire curriculum completed, Masato's party graduated, and to celebrate this, a large party was being held in their classroom. As a concession to their classmates, who were unable to graduate, it was officially being called a good-bye party, but either way, it was going to be quite a shindig.

Well, that had been the hope.

"…The game classes were all over the place, so why was the test totally normal? That's hardly fair…"

"…Questions from history, math, and English, all at our actual grade levels… What a nightmare…"

The test the day before had made Masato and Wise crave death, and they were sitting cross-legged in a corner of the class, sulking about it.

Their scores on the test were converted directly into bonus points—in theory, an extravagant amount of extra credit.

At any rate, their final SP scores: **Masato: 103 SP. Wise: 72 SP. Porta: 170 SP.**

The accumulative results of the first four days, plus the SP obtained normally through level-ups on the field trip, and then the test scores on top of that… Clearly, two of them had failed hard. It had naturally taken the wind out of their sails.

But what was done was done.

"Now, now, Ma-kun, Wise! Cheer up!" Mamako said, carrying dishes in both hands. "You both did your best. That's what really matters! You both did just fine! Let's celebrate!"

"Mama's cooking is all done! It's delicious!" Porta had sauce on her cheek. She must have stolen a bite.

"I helped! Let's all eat it together! Bwa-ha-ha!" Mr. Burly said. He had lapsed back into the diner-child routine, but best to ignore it.

The classroom desks were shoved together and soon covered in sushi and steak and deluxe sandwiches and cake. Quite the gourmet party smorgasbord if you don't get hung up on whether any of it went together.

And just in time, Medhi and Medhimama arrived, arms laden with grocery bags.

"Sorry we're late!"

"We brought drinks and snacks. I hope it's enough."

And with that, preparations were complete.

It all smelled too good to ignore. "…Well, we did get a lot of SP." "Yeah. It wasn't a complete loss."

And with that, Masato and Wise picked themselves up, and everyone raised a glass.

""""""Cheers!""""""

They ate, drank, and made merry with classmates they never did learn to distinguish (thanks to the ASCII art faces). This went on for a while.

Once things started to die down, Mamako came over to Masato. "Perhaps it's about time." "Yeah, I guess so." They'd discussed this beforehand. Masato had a job to do now.

As a final check, he looked to Wise and Porta in turn. Porta nodded vigorously. Wise gave a "suit yourself" shrug. He took that as agreement.

And as the party's representative, Masato went over to Medhimama.

"Medhimama, do you have a minute?"

"Oh? What is it?"

"If you don't mind…would you two like to join our party?"

"Huh? …You're inviting Medhi and me to join you?"

"Yes. I thought it would be great to have you with us. We're kind of a mess of a party, really, what with the lack of designated healer… Oh, but I'm not just after Cura, here. I think it would be fun to adventure with you."

Honestly, he was also worried about how Medhimama would deal with Medhi in the future, and that was definitely part of the offer.

Now he had to wait and see how Medhimama responded.

"I appreciate the offer, but I'm afraid I can't accept. Sorry."

That was a no. Masato had been turned down by a woman with a child. Shame.

"Uh… I can't change your mind, then?"

"Yes. For me, at any rate. I'm actually planning to log out after this."

"Log out…? You mean you're quitting?"

"Not permanently. I'm just going to take a break. I think I'll go back to the real world for a while. I need to take care of the unfortunate blog I'd filled with my parenting theories. I wouldn't want anyone following that and ending up like us."

"I see…"

"Which means I can't accept your offer, but Medhi… Well, I can hardly speak for her. Medhi, what would you like to do?" Medhimama asked, smiling gently. "This is your choice to make."

Medhi turned to Masato, with a far-too-beautiful smile.

"I'd be honored to accompany you. Thank you so much for inviting me."

On the surface, an unmistakably beautiful girl. A healer with a hidden dark power. Handy with a blunt instrument.

Add Medhi to the party?

"Yeah… Maybe you being my heroine is a bit unrealistic, but I'd gladly have you in my party." He grinned.

"Masato! You can't say that with a smile! I'm going to do everything I can to be your heroine! Just you wait!"

She took hold of her arms, deliberately pressing her chest against him. "See? You like this, right?" A sentence a prim and proper heroine would never utter.

But either way, **Medhi joined the party.**

"Well, there you have it. Um, but…isn't there some rule that parents and children have to play this game together? Is it okay if you stay here on your own?"

"Don't worry. Wise established precedent, so I'll take care of permissions."

"Eeek, where'd you come from?!"

A nun had manifested before him. Shiraaase.

She bowed her head to everyone, and then quickly began stuffing her face.

"Well, with everything neatly wrapped up," she announced once she'd finished eating, "all that remains is to give out the enhancement items you've been waiting for."

"Oh! That's right! They're the whole reason we came here, yet I totally forgot about them."

"HELL YEEEEAAAHHHH!!! The Prevenire will be miiiiiiiiiiiiiiiine!" Wise bellowed, immediately back in obnoxiously enthused mode, but she cooled off a moment later. "Oh, but…I only got seventy-two points. Is that gonna be enough to exchange for an ultra-rare item like a Prevenire?"

"Seventy-two points will be plenty. You can pull on the *gacha* seven times."

Shiraaase raised a hand, and a magic circle appeared.

"Just touch the magic circle, at a cost of ten SP a pull. And then, like magic, wonderful items will be yours."

"…Um, Shiraaase. I was sort of assuming that we could *directly* exchange the points we'd earned for the *specific* items we wanted. But…instead we've got a gacha?"

"Yes. A gacha."

The flyer had said they *could* get the items, not that they *would*. If they were in the gacha somewhere, it wasn't actually a lie. Shiraaase seemed to be calmly sticking to that official administrative position.

"Can I hit her?" Wise asked, fist at the ready.

"Better not," Masato said, restraining her.

Then Porta, unable to wait, stepped forward. Beaming with excitement.

"Um! Um! I'd like to try!"

"Oh, the top batter's Porta, then? Go right ahead. Good children get good results, you know. Heh-heh-heh."

"Then I'll try! C'mon!"

Ten SP vanished from Porta's window, and she touched the magic circle. Then...

Porta obtained Stuffed Animal!

"Wow! I got it! The Stuffed Animal! That's just what I wanted!"

Porta threw her arms around the Stuffed Animal (a cat) with a huge smile. That smile was all the reward anyone needed.

"As you can see, the desired results are possible. If anyone else would care to try..."

"Well... What do you think, Wise?"

"I want to, but I don't... These things never pay out. And we'd be trying our luck right after a jackpot... Nghhh... Oh, I know! Medhi, you try! Just once is fine!"

"No, I'd rather not. I'd prefer to use the points to raise my stats normally."

"That's definitely the smart option. The right decision. What are you gonna do, Masato?"

"I'm gonna play it safe and go for stat boosts, too."

"Argh, Masato! Don't be so boring! Are you sure that's what you want? Are you sure this isn't the time to test your luck? Coward! You're barely a man! A real man would never make the safe choice!"

"Argh, you talked me into it. Okay, then! I'll show you what I got! One hundred SP, all at once! Ten gacha pulls! Watch and weep!"

Masato blew all his SP on the gacha. He touched the magic circle, and the results…

Masato obtained HP + Drink ×10.

"Congratulations! As a hero, Masato already had very high HP, but you've received ten consumable items that raise your HP by a very small amount! That's basically a total wash."

"Noooooooooooooo! I should never have puuuuuuuulled!"

He chugged the drinks, tears streaming down his face. So salty.

With a sidelong glance at the weeping hero, Wise stepped forward with confidence.

"Heh-heh-heh! Since Masato blew it, I'm sure to score! That prize is mine! It must be mine! Breathe in…breathe out… Okay. Gimme seven! C'moooooon!"

Wise struck the gacha! The results!

Wise obtained MP + Drink ×7.

"Congratulations! As a Sage, Wise already had very high MP, but you've received seven consumable items that raise MP by a very small amount! You've self-destructed magnificently."

"Noooooooooooooo! I should never have puuuuuuuulled!"

But Wise downed all the drinks anyway. Good girl!

"Now, that's the end of rewards time…or it would be, but since you all fought very hard to protect parent-child bonds this time, we'll allow a single free pull as a reward. What do you say?"

"We have to at this point! This can't end with us getting nothing! Arghhh!"

"Ah, Masato, no fair!"

Who cared what Wise said? Masato jumped to the gacha magic circle, yelled, "I love you, admiiiiiiins!" and put his whole body into a dramatic touch! The result!

Mamako obtained Mom-Exclusive Apron.

"…Huh?"

"Oh my!"

"Oh, that is impressive! A mom-exclusive item from a child-targeted gacha! Mamako's mom luck is clearly beyond divine! My respect."

She could not be more obvious if she tried. She was infooormatively obvious.

This was clearly not a coincidental gacha result but always intended to gift Mamako an item only she could use. Masato was sure of it.

Masato was ready to put his entire soul into an angry protest, but...

"That means Ma-kun got a present for Mommy? Oh, how lovely! Thank you. I'll treasure it always! Hee-hee-hee."

Mamako tried the apron on, her smile so blinding, her joy so evident...

...that Masato just couldn't be that upset about it.

"...Well, as long as you're happy," he muttered, avoiding her eyes.

Afterword

Hello, dear reader. This is Inaka.

I really appreciate you picking up this book. I was able to release a second volume because of all of you. My gratitude is from the heart.

This is a story about parents and children. While writing it, I frequently encountered great difficulty.

The biggest challenge comes from just how many things can't be made perfectly clear.

Children are frustrated with their parents but can't bring themselves to completely reject them. There's always a part of them they can't bring themselves to hate...and a fear of what would happen if their mothers gave up on them.

Because of that, the children's attitudes can often end up feeling murky.

Meanwhile, the parents have their own issues; they have their own thoughts about parenting, based on their life experiences and values. As a mere writer, who am I to pass judgment on their ideas?

You see, what we have there is not right and wrong but merely differences of opinion. Just as each household puts different ingredients in their miso soup. As long as they enjoy the soup, they can put whatever they like in it! And that makes stories about parenting rather difficult.

I hope you will continue to support me in my efforts to wrangle the subject. Nothing would make me happier.

There are a few people I should thank.

Iida Pochi., who drew the illustrations. My publishers, my editor, K. Everyone involved in sales. You've all been such a great help. I can't thank you enough, and I ask that you continue to assist me.

*   *   *

Finally, I received a Valentine's Day message from Mother Inaka.
It read:

Dear Machida Inaka.
I got you no chocolate, just chocolate-like feelings.
Love,
Original Mom.

That's how she signed it...your classic mom e-mail. Thank you so
much.

Early spring 2017, Dachima Inaka

NEXT TIME

"Ma-kun, let's run a guild branch together!"

Get used to hearing "Come on in!" and "Welcome back!" because…
Mom's opening a guild branch?!

With their new party member, Medhi, their real adventure was just beginning…

But for some reason, Masato's party ends up operating a guild branch instead!

Faced with malicious complaints, salesmen peddling suspicious merchandise, constant staff shortages, and more, will they be able to turn a profit?!

A cutting-edge momcom adventure!
This time it's the guild arc!

VOLUME 3
ON SALE SUMMER 2019